THREE VERMARS, tall and reedy aliens who looked a lot like man-sized centipedes balanced on their tails, stood next to a water cooler, shooting the breeze. They spoke Vermararian, which always sounded to Kay like a cross between Esperanto and microphone feedback. And they smelled like fresh doughnuts.

Iggy, the senior of the triad, waved a pseudopod at Kay as he went to get coffee.

"How they floating, Iggy? Damn, don't tell me we're out of cream again? All we got is this powdered shit?"

Iggy chittered. Pointed at the counter.

"Oh, yeah, thanks. I didn't see it." He found the cream behind a box of stale doughnuts. "Thanks, Iggy."

Kay poured some cream into his coffee, stirred it, then looked at Edwards. "Okay, kid, you ready to roll?"

Edwards stood there with his mouth open, staring. Kay nodded at the Vermars. "See you around, guys."

They gave him some feedback squeals and waved.

Kay walked to where Edwards stood. Put one finger under his chin and pushed his mouth closed. "For future reference, this is a better look for you," he said. "Besides, some of our clients take that open mouth as a threat, you know?"

Edwards looked at him.

"C'mon, kid. Let's go take a walk. I'll fill you in on what you need to know."

MIB
MEN IN BLACK™

a Novel by
STEVE PERRY

Based on the Screen Story
and Screenplay by

ED SOLOMON

BANTAM BOOKS
New York   Toronto
London   Sydney   Auckland

MEN IN BLACK

A Bantam Book / July 1997

All rights reserved.

ISBN: 0-553-57756-5

Published simultaneously in the United States and Canada

Bantam Books are published by Bantam Books, a division of Bantam Doubleday Dell Publishing Group, Inc. Its trademark, consisting of the words "Bantam Books" and the portrayal of a rooster, is Registered in U.S. Patent and Trademark Office and in other countries. Marca Registrada. Bantam Books, 1540 Broadway, New York, New York 10036.

For Dianne:
Best friend I ever had.

Acknowledgments

Books—at least the ones I write—are collaborative works. While I generally put the actual words into a computer and eventually through a printer onto the paper, there are always people who help, and without whom the book wouldn't get done.

Thanks for that help this time go to Tom Dupree and Cassie Goddard, at Bantam, and I'd also like to offer my appreciation to Jean Naggar and the women of her agency: Jessie Margolis, Peggy Lawlis, Frances Kuffel, Alice Tasman, Anne Engel, Jennifer Weltz, and Joan Lilly.

Thanks, folks.

SP

I wish I loved the human race;
I wish I loved its silly face;
I wish I liked the way it walks;
I wish I liked the way it talks;
And when I'm introduced to one
I wish I thought, *What jolly fun!*

—Sir Walter Raleigh

MEN IN BLACK

It was past midnight, and the state road was as quiet as the inside of a coffin buried a hundred years. The south Texas summer skies were filled with stars, though, pinpoints of light against the black curtain of a moonless night.

The south Texas skies were also filled with a couple million insects—moths, mosquitoes, lightning bugs, June bugs, flying weevils, stray roaches, no-see-ums, and God knew what else. The bodies of a whole truckload of the suckers formed a gooey green and yellow paste on the windshield of the black '86 Ford LTD where it sat parked next to a clump of something that might—if it was lucky—grow up to be a tumble-weed someday. The car was on a tiny hillock a couple hundred yards off the road, but the ground was hard and dry, only a little sand sprinkled over it. Easy enough for even a stock Ford

1

to navigate on it. Not that the LTD was exactly stock . . .

A mosquito buzzed from the hot night in through the Ford's open passenger window.

Riding shotgun, Dee swatted at the mosquito, "Damned bugs."

Kay, the car's other occupant, sat behind the wheel, staring into the darkness. He said, "I hear that, partner."

Both men wore white shirts, black ties, and black suits. Their black shoes were so shiny they could have been patent leather.

Dee shook his head. He was the older of the two men, close to retirement age, and had a good fifteen years on Kay. "This is no way for a grown man to make a livin'," Dee said. He swatted at the mosquito again, smashed it against the side of his neck. Looked at the bloody spot on his palm with disgust, then wiped it on the windowsill.

"It's a dirty job, but somebody's got to do it," Kay said. He looked at a pack of Camels on the dash with longing. Be easier to do the job with a smoke. But— nope. Couldn't risk the light being seen. Maybe even smelled. Out here in the boonies, odors traveled a long way. Too bad.

"Sheeit. You and John Wayne. You gonna tell me a man's gotta do what a man's gotta do?"

"You wound me, Dee." Kay put a hand over his heart, as if shot. Glanced at the Camels again.

Dee caught the look. He shook his head again. "You keep smoking them cigarettes and you gonna wind up like the Duke did, too." He paused. "I'm gettin' too old for this, hoss."

They'd been partners a long time, they knew how

2

each other thought. "Ah, you're not old, you're just like a fine vintage wine, getting better with age."

"Turning into vinegar, you mean."

"Dee, Dee, why you want to talk like that . . . oops, *hel*-lo." Kay reached for the ignition key. "Looky here. It's *showtime*, folks."

In the flat distance, the lights of a lone vehicle gleamed on the state road.

"You gonna wait for the boys in green?"

"Just cranking the motor. But we want to time it right. Remember Canada?"

Dee smiled. "Oh, yeah. I thought I was going to throw an embolus I was laughing so hard. That Mountie. I wonder what ever happened to him?"

"Hell, he's probably running the country by now."

"Wouldn't surprise me at all," Dee said.

The Ford's engine caught with a rumble that was a lot more muscular than it ought to be for standard Detroit iron.

As they watched, several sets of auto headlights flared on the road to their left. The vehicles, a couple of 4WD's and late model Chevrolets colored a sickly, puke green, were lined up, blocking the road. They were close enough for Kay to read the INS logos on them.

La Migra, they called them down here.

The Border Patrol was awake and about to stem the tide of wetbacks. He grinned. Bush-league guys. They didn't have a clue; still, Kay felt a certain kinship with them. Such that it was.

The approaching vehicle slowed, came to a halt at the roadblock. Kay saw that it was a white van, couple years old, covered with dust that had surely spent the morning in Mexico.

Welcome to the Estados Unidos, amigos. Everybody out of the car and nobody moves real quick.

Kay put the Ford in gear. "Hi, ho, Silver," he said. He looked at Dee and grinned again.

"You call me Tonto and I'm gonna kick your sorry ass," Dee said.

Kay chuckled as he hit the accelerator.

The big Ford's tires spun and threw dirt.

The car headed toward the road.

"Hang on!" Kay said. He tromped the brake, cut the wheel, and put the LTD into a slide. Kicked up a lot of dust as the Ford skidded sideways and came to a stop behind the white van, both cars lit by the headlights of the Border Patrol's vehicles.

There were half a dozen INS boys—well, figuratively speaking, since one of them was a woman—spread out around the van. The Ford's arrival spooked them some, since about half of them pulled their pieces. Spooked too the dozen allegedly illegal Mexican immigrants standing behind the van where they were waiting for La Migra to finish busting their coyote before they all got sent back home. Life was hard. And expensive, too.

Dee and Kay got out of the Ford. "Evening, gentlemen," Kay said. He held up his badge case with its ID so nobody would get trigger happy. "We'll take it from here."

A tall good-looking kid of about thirty marched over to where Kay stood, shined his black aluminum six-cell light at Kay's ID. Squinted at it. "I'm agent Janus," the kid said. "This is my operation. Who the hell are—?"

He finally made out the ID. "*You're* INS?"

"Division Six," Kay said. He pocketed the badge case.

"I never *heard* of Division Six!"

"Really? You need to pay more attention to the memos from HQ, son. We selectively monitor field operations."

"Nobody told me—"

"I'm glad to hear that, 'cause if they had, they'd be in a lot of trouble. These little inspections are supposed to be a surprise. Now you stand back and let us have a few words with these folks."

It was all in your attitude, Kay knew. Act like you were in charge and nine times out of ten, whoever was on the scene would let you take over without much of a fight. The tenth time? Well, there were ways around that, if you were who Kay was.

The Mexicans stood in a line nervously, a group ranging in age from a babe in arms to a couple of grannies.

"What do you think, Dee?"

Dee walked along the line, looking carefully at the illegals. "Tough call. Guess we're going to have to do it the old-fashioned way."

Kay nodded. He moved to the first man in line, a tall man in jeans and a T-shirt and tire sandals. "¿Qué pasa, amigo, cómo se llama?" *What's happenin' pal? What's your name?*

"Miguel," the man said.

Kay smiled, moved on. To one of the grannies, he said, "No se preocupe, abuela. Bienvenida a los Estados Unidos." *Don't worry, grandmother, welcome to the U.S.*

"Gracias, señor," she said.

He kept up a patter of liquid Spanish as he went down the line, smiling and nodding at the group. How are you? What is your name? Where are you going? Welcome to the U.S.

When he got to the fifth man, who smiled like an idiot, Kay turned and glanced at Dee, who nodded. Definitely possible. To the man, Kay said, still in Spanish, "Hey, friend, what say I break your face?"

The man's smile stayed pasted on and he nodded.

Kay and Dee exchanged glances. Dee said, "Maybe he's just a masochist? You know, into pain?"

"I know what a masochist is," Kay said.

"You don't understand a word of this, do you, friend?" Kay said, still using Spanish.

The man smiled and nodded.

Some of the other illegals frowned at their comrade. From his appearance, the man was obviously not of pure Indio blood, so he should certainly be able to understand what La Migra had just said and it was apparent he did not.

One of the grannies made the sign of the cross.

"Ah, folks, I do believe we have a winner," Kay said, glancing at Dee yet again. In Spanish, he said, "The rest of you are free to go. Back into the van and scram."

Janus, not unexpectedly, took exception. "*What?* You can't do that!"

"Son, I can do just about anything I want here. This is a special Division Six operation and if you give me any flack, you're gonna be riding a swaybacked donkey down on the Rio Grande for the next five years where the most exciting thing you'll see all day will be a lizard taking a leak."

Janus paled, visible even in the dim light.

All in the attitude. Act like you have the power, people believe you.

The van's driver didn't wait to see who had the bigger cojones. He jumped into the van, yelled at his passengers, who piled into the back. The van pulled around the roadblock and sped north.

"This is highly irregular!" Janus tried.

"Agent Janus, is it? A man who hasn't been able to take a dump for four days is highly irregular. We do this kind of thing all the time. Now, you run along and let us deal with Paco here. And keep this to yourselves. We like to maintain a low profile in Division Six."

The INS stood their ground.

Kay said, "Go on. Up to now, your files are clean. Don't make me have to send a memo to your chief."

The moment held, but Kay had shooed away stronger men than Janus here.

Janus broke. Muttered something under his breath, probably obscene. Kay kept his face stern.

Reluctantly, Janus and the other agents headed for their vehicles.

Once they were gone, Dee and Kay looked at their captive. "This way, amigo," Kay said. "We need to have a few words with you."

From beneath his coat, Dee pulled what looked like a Desert Eagle in .44 mag and waved it at the captive. A major handgun, the Israeli piece, even the stock ones, and this one didn't look quite like the basic out-of-the-box model. It had a few modifications.

Quite *unusual* modifications, at that.

It was apparent that the illegal immigrant either understood English or the meaning of a big old gun pointing at him. He moved off the road and behind a couple of creosote bushes with the two men.

Kay put an arm around the man's shoulders. "I think maybe you jumped off the bus in the wrong part of town, amigo. In fact, I'd bet dollars against pesos you're not from anywhere *remotely* near here."

With that, Kay pulled the electronic stripper from his belt and triggered it, ran it down the front of the immigrant's clothes. The laser light flashed and there came a sound much like somebody undoing a heavy zipper.

The immigrant's clothes peeled away from his body.

Then his *flesh* peeled away from his body.

What remained was a five-and-a-half-feet-tall creature covered with scales, snail-like tentacles, and eyes mounted on stalks. The only bit of camouflage remaining was the immigrant's head, mounted on a stick held in the creature's tentacles. The fake head continued to smile and nod as the alien operated the controls on the other end of the rod.

Kay shook his head. "Mikey? When did they let *you* out of jail?"

The alien made a reply. It sounded like a combination of a lizard eating a moth and a jar full of angry wasps.

Kay smiled. "Political refugee? Uh-huh, right. Do I look like I was born yesterday, Mikey?"

Dee said, "You know how many treaty articles you've just violated?"

Mikey gave out a lame squeak.

Dee said, "Well, let's see. Unauthorized immigration, failure to document inoculations, nonpayment of landing fee, failure to obtain a proper visa—ah, Mikey, Mikey, the list goes on and on. You in a lot of trouble, boy."

Kay said, "Yep, and whoever dropped you in old May-he-co is gonna owe you a refund. At the very least, you should have gotten a language implant or one of them contraband universal translators. Can't trust anybody these days, can you, Mikey?"

Mikey sputtered more noise—crunched a few moths, tried to rid himself of a few irritated wasps.

"Now, now, you know better than that. Don't insult us here, Mikey. That won't do you any good. You don't really want to add bribery to the charges, do you?" Kay said.

Mikey shut up. Smartest thing he'd done all day.

"Hand me the head and put out your tentacles. You know the drill," Kay ordered.

"Good God!" somebody said from behind them.

Kay and Dee turned, as did Mikey.

In the starlight, Agent Janus stood there gaping at them.

"Well . . . shit," Kay said.

Mikey dropped the animaelectronic puppet head and snarled, showing an impressive array of large sharklike teeth that didn't seem to go with his diminutive frame. He could take off a man's arm with fangs like that.

The stench of his breath was like meat that had rotted a few days in the hot Texas sunshine. Kay was used to stinks of various kinds, but Mikey could use a couple gallons of Listerine, that was for sure.

Agent Janus screamed as the alien slammed into Dee, knocked him sprawling, then took off—

—straight for Janus.

The INS agent tried to pull his gun, fumbled the weapon, then dropped it.

Mikey bounded toward the man, emitted a

10

scream that started high and scaled right into the ultrasonic.

Janus stood there like a rabbit caught in a Mack truck's headlights, paralyzed with fear, his brain obviously unable to believe what his eyes were telling it: *Look, it's a land shark coming to eat you! My, my.*

"Mikey, stop!" Kay yelled. That didn't help, the little bastard kept on charging. What the hell had gotten into him? Mikey wasn't violent, at least he hadn't ever been before. Who did he think Janus was?

Dee rolled to his hands and knees, cursed, picked up the gun he'd dropped, cursed, adjusted a control on the side, cursed again.

Kay went for his own weapon but he didn't know if he could clear leather in time to make the shot. Mikey had up a good head of steam by now.

"Dee! Shoot!" he yelled. But Dee was still fiddling with his gun's controls—

Kay jerked his gun from the hip holster under his jacket but it came out with glacial slowness. . . .

Time stalled, like a car hitting a Mississippi mudflat and sinking up to the axles. Dammit—!

Mikey sprinted the last few yards, gathered himself for the leap, and sprang—

Kay lined up, no time for sights! and fired—

Mikey's torso exploded into hot blue goo as a sizzling white flash speared him. Bits of tissue and circulating fluid sprayed like a burst water balloon, painting the landscape and the terrified INS agent alike with dead Mikey.

The alien fell, tumbled, sprawled next to Janus, dead before he slid to a stop.

Kay blew out a big sigh. Damn. That was close. He

kept his weapon out, did a fast three-sixty out of habit, looking for more targets. No more like Mikey, but he saw the rest of the INS boys hopping out of their cars, heard doors slamming and yelling as they ran toward the flash and noise.

Now there was *really* a stink to complain about. Peuwee!

"Well, *shit*," Kay said. He put his gun away.

At least Mikey wasn't going to be sneaking on-planet any more.

Dee came to his feet, shook his head, holstered his own weapon.

Janus, pale as a room full of Republicans in Georgia, tried to speak:

"Th—Th—Th—"

"That?" Kay offered.

"Wa—Wa—Wasn't—Wasn't—"

"Human?" Kay finished. "I know. Here, you got some entrail on you." Kay reached over with his hand-kerchief and brushed away some of the goo that had recently been Mikey. "That ought to come right out with a little soda water. Or Spray 'n' Wash on the cold cycle."

The other INS agents boiled in, bristling with guns and questions.

"What the hell is going on—?"

"—Agent Janus, are you okay—?"

"—hell *is* that thing—?"

"Take it easy, everybody," Kay said, using his best authoritarian voice. "The situation is under control here, just calm down. If you'll give me your attention for a moment I will explain everything."

Janus was still in shock but there were a lot of people waving guns and looking at the late and—Kay had to admit—unlamented Mikey, whose real name was unpronounceable by anything with human vocal cords. He was not going to be wasting anybody's time anymore, except to clean him up and dispose of him.

Kay sighed. Well. They'd stepped in it now. And where the hell *was* the cleanup crew? He looked around.

As if in response to the thought, a pair of headlights approached on the road, fast, the roar of the car's engine loud in the desert night. "About damned time," Kay said.

A uniformed agent pointed his somewhat shaky pistol at Kay. "You better do some fast talking, mister! There's no such thing as an INS Division Six!"

"If I may?" Kay said. He put his hand into his inside coat pocket—slowly—and pulled the neuralyzer out, also very slowly. Held it up for the man covering him to see. It didn't look threatening. What it looked like was a pocket recorder with a red diode on it. He glanced at his watch, then at the neuralyzer, did the math, then set the counter. If the cleanup crew had to hurry, well, that was their problem. Teach them to be dragging in that way.

The kid with the gun said, "What the hell is that?"

"Mikey? The species name wouldn't mean anything to you—oh, you mean *this*? Well, son, it's a neuralyzer. A gift from some . . . out-of-town friends. The little red eye here isolates and measures bioelectric impulses in your brain. Actually, to be more specific, it works on the ones connected to your memory. Once those are stored, then things are a snap."

"What the hell are you talking about?" the kid said.

The car approaching pulled to a halt. Some of the INS team turned to face it, guns drawn.

The cleanup crew, six men, dressed in identical black

suits, white shirts, black ties, and mirror-bright black shoes, alighted from the car. Another '86 LTD, also black. The six already had their sunglasses on.

Kay called out to the men in black: "We're gonna need a splay burn on the perimeter, gentlemen, holes at forty, sixty, and eighty, if you would be so kind, as we play the old underground gas pocket routine yet again."

Janus found his voice. "If you don't explain what is going on here, right now, I'm hauling all your asses in!"

"Take it easy, I'm about to."

"Who *are* you?"

"Well, son, I'm afraid I'm just a figment of your imagination. And that not for long."

Kay pulled his sunglasses from his handkerchief breast pocket, saw Dee do the same. The two men put the glasses on. "Everybody, look here," Kay said. He waved the neuralyzer.

All the agents looked. They'd have done so if he had told them *not* to look at it. All in all, humans were a pretty gullible species. And pretty predictable, most of the time.

Kay triggered the device. There came a brilliant strobelike flash. Kay looked at his watch. "Like I said, better hurry, gentlemen."

Quickly, the six men in black went back to their Ford's trunk and pulled out flamethrowers. They fired several blasts, set burning blobs of fuel in a circular pattern around Kay, Dee, and the Border Patrol guys. And gal. The INS agents didn't move. The men in black hurriedly put the flamethrowers away, pulled fire extinguishers from the car's trunk, and stood ready.

There was a lot of room inside an '86 LTD's trunk. He glanced at his watch again. They could move pretty damned fast when they had to, Kay had to give them that.

Right about . . . now . . .

Janus said, "Huh? What the hell—?"

"Seems to be the question of the night, doesn't it? Lucky to be alive after a blast like that, aren't we, fellas?"

The other INS agents came out of their trances. Looked around, puzzled.

The men in black sprayed extinguisher foam on the burning spots.

"Is that a freak accident or what?" Kay said. "Who'd ever figure there was a pocket of underground gas out here? You need to be more careful discharging your firearms when you smell gas, son. Could have killed us all."

After the INS boys and girl had departed, new memories in place, and the cleanup crew had also booked, Kay walked back to the LTD. Dee sat on the hood, idly swatting at mosquitoes, his sunglasses dangling from one hand. Kay leaned against the car's door.

"How're you doin', Dee?"

"I'm sorry about back there," Dee said. "Mikey should have never gotten the jump on me like that."

"Hey, it happens."

"It didn't used to. Ten years ago, I'd have plugged him before he twitched. Even five years ago, I could have hit him before he took three steps." He held up his hands. They trembled. "I'm past it, Kay."

Kay didn't say anything. He could feel his partner's pain.

Dee looked up. "Beautiful, aren't they? The stars. We just don't look at them much anymore."

"Easier to see out here in the middle of nowhere," Kay said. "No city glow, no smog, no buildings in the way."

"Yeah."

For a long moment, neither man said anything.

"We had some good times, didn't we? Took care of business?"

"That we did."

"I'll tell you, Kay, I know it's time to go, but I am going to miss the chase." He waved at the smoldering spots in the desert.

Kay already had the neuralyzer out, down by his leg where Dee couldn't see it. He felt a great wave of sadness wash over him. He put on his sunglasses.

"No," he said quietly. "You're not gonna miss it at all, Dee."

The silver shield on its chain around his neck thumped against James Edwards's chest as he ran through the New York City night, whacking him pretty good, given as how it was just a badge and not all that heavy.

Probably be a little bit heavier if it was gold, but there wasn't much chance of *that* happening any time soon. It was kind of hard to get to be detective when you had an attitude like James, even he had to admit that. Still, the silver one was whacking him hard enough.

Of course, he was running full speed. And even though they'd left the two out-of-shape uniforms in the dust behind them, the fleeing perp held his lead over Edwards. The man was twenty-five yards ahead and going strong. Christ, the perp must be some kind of track star, though he sure didn't look it. Edwards himself was the

3

fastest guy he knew, and he'd normally have run nine out of ten bad guys down by now, especially working undercover and getting to wear his running shoes. The perp must be on something. Speed. Or ginseng or vitamins or something.

Well, he'd been chasing the guy for six blocks in the damned dark and this was getting old. He had already worked up a real sweat and it was way, way too hot for this crap.

The perp ducked into the subway. Right into Grand Central Terminal.

Fine.

Time to try something else.

"Stop! NYPD!" he yelled. Sometimes that helped.

It helped, all right.

The perp fired his afterburners and put on a burst of speed.

This is *not* how to get your gold shield, James, he told himself mentally. You don't let them outrun you.

Few people in the station bothered to look at the running men. This was New York City, after all. Everybody had seen stranger things, usually every day of the week and probably twice on Sunday. Cop chasing a perp? Not enough interest for the average ten-year-old to worry about.

"Stop! Police!" he tried again.

The perp just sped up more.

Damn, Edwards thought. Better save his breath for running.

Oops. Look out, the perp was heading up and back to the streets again.

Taking the stairs two at a time, Edwards continued his pusuit.

A cab screeched to a rubber-burning stop inches away

from slamming into the sprinting detective, and the driver expressed an opinion as to Edwards's IQ.

"Yeah, yeah," Edwards said. He offered a one-fingered salute to the cabbie in response and kept running.

The perp made it to Park Avenue Bridge. He looked back at Edwards, then vaulted over the rail to Forty-first Street below.

Damn, that was a thirty-foot drop, easy! Guy had to be tanked on something!

Edwards took as deep a breath as he could get and bailed over the side. Perp could do it, *he* could do it—

Oof—! He came down on one of those cheesy fake double-decker buses. This one was full of tourists. Enough cameras among them to sink the Staten Island Ferry. They gaped at him openmouthed.

"Don't worry folks, just part of the tour."

Perp! Where was the perp—!

There he was. Already off the bus and on his feet again. Damn!

One of those slow-moving *New York Post* delivery trucks came by. Going in the right direction. Edwards sprinted, caught the back of the truck, climbed aboard.

There the perp was, running along the curb. Still going strong, too.

The truck caught up with the perp. Edwards leaned out and smiled. "End of the line, pal. Your luck just ran out!"

He jumped from the truck and brought the perp down with a fairly nice tackle, if he did say so himself.

The perp yelled, "He's coming! He's coming!"

Edwards shook his head. "Yeah, right. He gets here, I'm gonna bust his ass, too. Gimme your hands."

He pulled his cuffs.

The perp turned his face toward the policeman. He looked terrified.

Then he blinked, and Edwards pulled his face back and stared at the perp.

Holy shit!

The guy had *two sets of eyelids!* The outside ones were normal, but the inside ones were white and kind of gummy looking. Euuyew!

Something was definitely wrong with this picture.

"He's coming! He's coming!" the perp babbled again.

"Who you talking about? Jesus? Don't worry, you gonna be in a nice safe cell when he gets here, we'll send him around to see you and the other sinners—"

Abruptly, the perp moved. He had something in his hand.

Gun!

It was a weird-looking piece, like it belonged on Deep Space Nine or Babylon Five or somewhere, but there was no mistaking what the perp was gonna do with it. He pointed it at Edwards. The gun's bottom half glowed a kind of pulsing yellow and it whined like a dog whistle.

Must be one of them new laser jobs, probably had an infrared sight or something on it. Gee-zus—!

NYPD on-undercover-assignment officer James Edwards focused his entire attention on that weird gun the perp pointed at him. That was where the danger was and he couldn't really see much but that big gun. He grabbed the perp's hand and slammed it down against the street.

The perp's gun went poof! and shattered into a million pieces, zap, just like that.

Son of a . . . !

The perp slammed his knee into Edwards's groin.

Oh, *man*!

Edwards grunted in pain, released his grip on the man. Grabbed at his injury.

The perp took off like his tail was on fire.

Felt like part of him was on fire, too, but now he was really pissed. Nobody was going to give him a groin shot and just *leave,* thank you very much!

Edwards put the pain into a holding area and started after the perp again. This guy sure was going to a lot of effort to avoid a bust for what would probably get bargained down to a misdemeanor. Didn't make any sense.

Most of what criminals did didn't make any sense.

"Goddammit! You *stop!* You're making me mad here!"

Then the perp leaped *over* a moving car and ran toward the Guggenheim.

Edwards stared. Nobody in the world could make that kind of jump!

A bus rolled in front of him and Edwards pulled up short.

When the bus passed, there was no sign of the perp.

Well, *damn*!

Edwards was in good shape but he wasn't planning on running a marathon and breaking the world's high-jump record when he clocked in this shift.

Edwards got to the Guggenheim and leaned over the wall that surrounded it, looking for his quarry—

Something flew past him. The perp, who leaped from twenty feet down to the top of the Guggenheim.

Man!

This had to be a nightmare, it couldn't be real. But

even so, he wasn't going to let this guy get away now. He ran into the museum, up the grand ramp.

While he ran, he said to himself, "Man! I *knew* I shoulda called in sick and gone to the ball game!"

When the perp opened the roof door to go into the Guggenheim, he got a surprise.

"Hi, there, Spiderman," Edwards said, his pistol aimed at the perp's nose. "Tell you what, you teach me that jumping trick and I'll put in a good word for you at the trial."

The perp moaned and started to back away, his hands held out in front of him.

"Hold up there, pal."

But the perp kept backpedaling, until he reached the roof's edge again.

"No! He's coming! He'll kill me! I failed and he'll kill me!"

Edwards didn't know who "he" was, but it had dawned on him it probably wasn't Jesus—not unless he planned to come back a lot more militant than he'd gone out. "Take it easy, pal. Nobody is going to kill you. I know a nice safe place, got real thick padded walls, nobody can get to you there. You just come along with me, we'll protect you from him."

The perp tried to back up some more, but he was out of room. He hit the short safety wall—

—looked down, then back at Edwards—

—and went right over—

He screamed all the way down.

Edwards look over the side. He wasn't walking away from this fall.

"Damn, man, what the hell are you?"

I mean, *were* you, Edwards thought.

He leaned back. Heard sirens, but figured they weren't for him. The uniforms were back there somewhere, lost in the vastness of the city. He needed to find a phone and call this in. He really ought to consider popping for a cellular, never knew when he might really need it, but since he would only use it on the job, it didn't seem right he should have to pay for it.

Boy, this wasn't gonna go over big back at the precinct.

No, sir, he could already hear the shoofly they'd send over, see his surprised expression.

Should have stayed home in bed this shift, no two ways about it, James, my man.

James Edwards sat on one of the seen-better-days plastic chairs in Interrogation 1. So far, his expectations about this meeting had been fulfilled. In spades.

The room smelled of stale cigarette smoke and unwashed criminals, even though smoking in the building had been against the rules for a couple of years now. Stinky perps weren't covered by departmental policy. Too bad.

Across from the young cop was the inspector from IAD. The shoofly, as regular cops like to call them. They were called other names, too, but most of those couldn't be used in polite company.

Not that polite company was apt to gather in this rathole of a room.

The inspector said, "Two sets of eyelids. You mean he blinked with both eyes?"

"No, sir, I mean he had one set and then he blinked with another set. Inner and outer lids. Sir."

The fat sergeant said, "Kind of like, low beams and high beams?"

Edwards glared at the fat sergeant, one of the two uniforms who'd been behind him when he'd started chasing the perp—whatever the hell he was.

The inspector from Internal Affairs cleared his throat. "Let's move on, shall we?"

He glanced down at the written report. Shuffled the papers. Considered his next words carefully.

"Was there anything else strange about the deceased suspect?"

"Other than he must have been training for the Olympics? This guy was the fastest thing on two feet I've ever seen. He was wearing regular street shoes, too."

"What size were they?" the sergeant said.

The inspector said, "You two want to bottle the by-play so we can get this thing finished?"

"Yeah, I hear you," Edwards said. "Sir."

"So, Officer Edwards, did these, ah, *eyelids* come out before or after the perpetrator drew the weapon that vanished in a puff of smoke when you hit it?"

Snide sucker, this guy. He didn't need to be sarcastic. "Before."

Inspector Shoofly glanced over at the fat sergeant and Phillips, the other uniform. Said, "And why is it, do you think, that these two officers did not see these . . . eyelids and goofy handgun?"

"Because they were coughing their smoked-up lungs out five blocks behind me, that's why. They didn't get any closer to him than I am to getting my gold shield." A long beat passed. "Sir."

25

The fat sergeant rolled his eyes. "Ah, Jimbo Edwards, light-years ahead of the rest of us, all by himself, that right? You aren't half the man I am!"

"That's true. You gotta outweigh me by a couple hundred pounds."

"Listen up, Edwards, you ever think that it might be *possible* that on the entire force there could be one or two guys besides you who aren't complete fools?"

What seemed like a long time passed.

"Edwards?"

"I'm still thinking about it."

"Smart mouth, just keep it up and see where it gets you. Just remember that next time you need backup."

"I was remembering it *this* time, Sarge. My backup was way back, probably thinking about their next doughnut and cigarette."

The fat sergeant flushed. Must have hit close to home, Edwards thought.

The other uniform spoke up. "Uh, look, Inspector, I just remembered why I didn't notice the guy's *eyelids*. I was too busy staring at those little *antennae* coming out the top of his head. I think he was sending signals to Mars to start the invasion, that's what I think. We should put in a call to the president, you know?"

The sergeant laughed.

The inspector frowned. "I think we're about done here." He closed his notebook, shook his head. "Sergeant, I'd like to speak to you and Officer Phillips outside, please." He got up, nodded at Edwards, headed for the hallway that led to the squad room. He stopped in front of the one-way mirror, paused and looked at himself, straightened his tie.

As he was leaving, the sarge said, "Listen up, Jimbo,

you want to get along, you got to go along. You need to cut out all this cowboy stuff. Try to be a team player."

"This team makes the Jets look good," Edwards said.

For a second, it looked as if the fat man might swing on him, but he held it down. Cops hitting other cops was very politically incorrect these days, no matter how much you might want to do it.

After they were gone, Edwards slumped in his chair. Man, this was crazy. Guy with two sets of eyelids, able to climb walls like a human fly. Maybe this was all a bad dream? Maybe somebody had slipped some acid into his coffee?

Okay, okay, so the guy was some kind of freak or something. He'd seen that show on the Nature channel or Discovery or PBS or somewhere, about those people in Spain or Portugal who only had two toes and two fingers on each hand. Double dactyl or something like that?

And there was the dog-faced boy and human alligators and fat ladies. Had to be a lot stranger people than one who could run like the wind and who had eyes like a frog or snake or something.

And who carried humming rayguns that shattered when you hit them hard? Probably all them superconductors.

So, how to explain all those things? Maybe it was like a *Star Trek* episode? Some weird space tornado kicked the *Enterprise* back in time, like it did every other week or so, and this guy was part of the crew. Or running from the crew.

Yeah, right.

He closed his eyes, feeling exhausted. Stuff like this wasn't supposed to happen. Way it was supposed to go was, the bad guys would do crime and he would catch them and throw 'em in the cage. Wasn't supposed to be stuff this weird happening, even in New York City.

Man, he was tired. All that running, then having IAD hammer away at him for what seemed like forever. Maybe he'd just rest his head on the scarred table for a minute. . . .

Almost before he knew it, Edwards felt himself drop off into sleep. . . .

He awoke when somebody touched him on the shoulder. He jerked, spun away from the touch—

A pretty good-looking woman in a lab coat stood there looking at him.

What, he'd died and this was his reward? Well, not bad, not bad.

"Officer Edwards?"

"Yeah?"

"I'm Laurel Weaver, deputy medical examiner. You sent us over a corpse this afternoon—"

"I didn't send him over, Doc, he sent himself."

"Whatever. Can you tell me something about it? I mean, its background."

" 'It?' "

She looked around, leaned closer to him. She looked tired, too, like maybe she'd been dragged out of bed and was six hours shy of a good night's sleep. "Yeah, well, I did a quick prelim, opened it up, and let me tell you, I've never seen anything—" she chopped off her words as the door to the interrogation room swung open and Heroumin, the Polish detective, peered in. "Somebody here to see you, James."

Edwards shook his head. Now what?

Heroumin moved off.

The doctor said, "Listen, I don't want to talk about this here. I have to go. Check by the morgue later, okay? I really think we should discuss this further." There was a sense of urgency in her speech.

"Uh, yeah, right." Well, why not? She was a lot better looking than his landlady, who was the only other woman he had any kind of relationship with at the moment. And that was limited to her pounding on his door either to ask for the rent or to tell him to turn his crummy music down.

"I'll call you, set up an appointment or something," he said.

"Please. And make it quickly. I have a strange feeling about this."

"I hear that," he said.

She left and he stared at her. Somebody stopped her just outside the door in the hallway, he couldn't see who, but he heard a man's voice say, "Ah, Dr. Weaver, from the coroner's office. You're working on that John Doe jumper, is that right?" The speaker had more than a little cracker in him, to judge from his voice.

"Yes, I'm Dr. Weaver. Why?"

"Look here, doctor."

"What is that?"

There came a bright flash of light, like a lightning strobe. What the hell? Edwards started for the door.

A man in a black suit and white shirt, wearing Ray·Ban shades, stepped in front of the door, blocking it. "Evening. You'd be Officer James Edwards, is that right?"

"I am. Who are you?"

The man in black walked to the videocam inside its steel cage in the corner. Pointed what looked like a penlight at it and pushed a button. There was a little hum and the videocam's red light went out. He pulled his shades off, pocketed them.

"Have a seat, son."

"I'm not your son and I'm done sitting for the time being. Who are you?"

"Call me Kay," the man said. "Some day, huh?"

Edwards glared at him, but didn't speak.

Kay smiled. "Want to tell me what happened out there?"

"You some kind of fed?"

"Something like that."

"How about I tell you a joke instead? You gonna laugh either way."

"Do I look like somebody with a sense of humor?"

"I dunno. Do I look like a lunatic? Ask anybody around here, my guess is that's what they'd tell you."

"Let me see. The guy who fell off the roof had two sets of eyelids, the inner set of which were kind of gummy looking?"

"How'd you know that?"

"The inner ones were gills."

"Gills? Like a fish?"

"In a manner of speaking. Let's just let that part slide for now."

"What else you know about this dude?"

"He jumped like he had his own trampoline on his feet?"

Edwards felt better. He wasn't crazy, and this dude right here was the proof. No, he had stumbled into something, something big enough to bring in the feds. Now, the trick was, how to find out what it was. And who this guy was.

"What are you? FBI?"

"You ran him down and then kicked his ass? That's pretty amazing, son, you don't know how amazing. I have to tell you, I am impressed and I don't impress all that easily."

"CIA? You know about this thing, don't you?"

"I know about a lot of things. Did he say anything before he fell?"

"Some kind of nonsense. Something like 'He's coming, I failed, he's gonna kill me!' shit like that."

"That's it?"

"That's it."

"This weapon he had, you think you'd recognize it if you saw it again?"

"Last time I saw it, it was busted into a million pieces. One jigsaw puzzle looks pretty much like the next one when it's unassembled."

"But you would recognize another one if it wasn't blowed up?"

"I'm a trained police officer. Yeah, I'd recognize it."

The man in black stood. Smiled, but it didn't touch his eyes. "Come on, let's take a little ride. I've cleared it with your lieutenant, you're being detached to help us in this matter."

"National Security Agency?"

The man in black just grinned wider.

Inside the LTD, Kay grinned as the young cop looked around.

"Come on, man, who you with? Can't be anybody with any money, you driving a piece of crap like this."

Kay said, "It's a good car."

"Oh, pardon me, I didn't mean to *offend* you. I mean, I guess I should have remembered an '86 Ford

LTD is a *classic* and all." He waved at the car. "Right up there with Cords and boat-tail speedsters and all. What, your other car is a Gremlin? A nice pink Rambler?"

"Things sometimes aren't what they seem," Kay said. "I'd have thought you'd have figured that out after today."

That shut him up for a second, then the kid said, "Well, I guess that means you *aren't* a guy who's been doing whatever it is you do for way too long, 'cause that's what you *seem* like to me. You look kinda burned out, you don't mind my saying so."

Kay admired the kid's perception, but he didn't say anything.

"Struck a chord, didn't I? That's my thing, I'm good on people."

"Are you?"

"Damn straight. So, who are you? Lay it out, Mr. Man in Black."

Kay said, "I work for an agency that monitors and polices alien activities here on Earth."

"That right? Uh-huh, yeah, sure, me, too, in fact—" he stopped as Kay pulled the LTD to the curb. He looked around. "This is not the best neighborhood, you know, to be stopping in. That's Jack Jeebs's pawnshop, guy buys from two-bit chain grabbers and purse snatchers, guys who break into tourist cars to swipe whatever is on the seat."

"I know."

"Dude doesn't deal in guns, you wasting your time here."

"Maybe not. Let's go in, shall we?"

"No skin off my ass. But I have to tell you, even a piece of junk like this Ford is gonna be half gone time we get back. They got boys that can strip it to the frame while you go in to take a leak."

"I have an alarm system."

"They can get around any alarm you got, pal. You must not be from around here—this is New York City. They can steal the gold out of your teeth while you waiting for the subway."

"I'll take my chances."

Edwards shrugged. "Your car. Don't say I didn't warn you."

Kay smiled again. He liked this kid. He was sassy, brash. Reminded him of himself twenty years or so ago. He walked around to the trunk, popped it. "Go ahead on in, let Jeebs know we want to have a few words with him, would you?"

"Right. Then you gonna tell me who you are?"

"If you really want to know."

Kay watched the kid swagger into the pawnshop. Shook his head. Ah, the arrogance of youth. He closed the trunk, pulled the the trigger device from his coat pocket, pointed it at the LTD, and pressed the arm button.

The Ford peeped at him.

He was almost to the door of the pawnshop before the first booster got to the Ford and tried to slim-jim the lock. There was a loud *pop!* and when Kay looked back, all that remained of the would-be car thief was a smoking, dark spot on the sidewalk.

He grinned. The longer they stayed inside, the safer the cars in this part of the city were going to get. Kay opened the door as he heard another *pop!* and grinned wider as he stepped into the pawnshop.

All in a day's work.

Jack Jeebs was a baggy-faced man who looked to be in his mid-forties. He wore clothes that looked as if he had gotten them from Rip Van Winkle after Rip's long sleep in them. Put the clothes on without washing them or even bothering to shake the wrinkles out, too. As Edwards entered the pawnshop—itself hardly the acme of modern civilization—Jeebs was throwing stuff into boxes, moving like a man in a big hurry.

Place smelled like a goat farm Edwards had once visited as a kid. Kind of place where you want to spray everything with Lysol before you touched it, and then wear rubber gloves and maybe rubber boots just in case.

"Going someplace, Jeebs?"

The pawnshop owner paused for a moment, looked up, then went back to loading the card-

5

board box. He threw a toaster into it. It *clanged* against a waffle iron. "Hey, Officer Edwards. Uh, yeah, I, uh, found a great deal on a place uptown. I'm . . . relocating. If it's any of your business."

Edwards drifted toward Jeebs. The harried man smelled as if he'd wandered into a skunk convention and each animal had paused to pay its respects to the man before moving on. This whole case stank to high heaven. "What is this I see?"

Edwards poked at a box of fake Rolexes.

Jeebs paused in his packing. "Oh, hey, geez, I was sure I turned those in to the proper authorities. I'll drop 'em off on my way uptown."

Edwards looked around, then back at the nervous little man. "Well, the fact is, Jeebs, I'm looking for something a little more esoteric than a box full of fake watches. You know what I'm talking about here?"

"Come on, Officer, you know I quit handling porno."

"I'm not talking about those pictures somebody scammed from *Penthouse*, Jack. I'm talking about something on the lines of hardware. Lethal hardware."

Jeebs paled. He swallowed, shook his head. "I don't know what you mean, Officer."

Edwards grinned. Jack might as well have a big flashing neon sign over his head saying, LYING SCUM HERE!

"I look stupid to you, Jeebs? Got the word 'Fool' tattooed on my forehead? You're hiding something. Of course, you're always hiding something. And inquiring minds want to know."

Jeebs's eyes went wide as he stared past Edwards.

Man looked like he'd just seen Dracula stroll into the joint. Edwards glanced over his shoulder.

Agent or Operative or Whatever-the-hell-he-was Kay had just stepped into the place. Edwards wondered if that was a first or a last name?

Jeebs said, "Uh . . . hiya, Kay."

Edwards frowned. Glanced back at Jeebs, then at Kay again. "You know this scumbag?"

"We're acquainted, yes," Kay said. "Okay, Jeebs, where are the imports?"

"Imports? I'm sure I don't know what you're talking about, Kay."

"Jeebs, Jeebs, why do you do this? Lie to me? After all we've been through?"

"You got it all wrong, Kay. I wouldn't shine you on."

"And it never rains in California, either." Kay pulled his pistol and pointed it at Jeebs. "You know what I do to liars, Jeebs?"

Edwards fought to keep his grin in check. He knew this routine.

Kay was bad cop. And he knew his part.

"Hey, take it easy, Kay. Jeebs is trying to help us here, ain't that right, Jeebs?"

Jeebs said nothing. He swallowed. He held another toaster in his hands, stared at Kay.

Kay said, "I'm going to count to three. If you don't give me what I want to see, I'm gonna blow your head off." He levered the hammer back on his pistol. Kept his face deadpan.

No subtlety, the man went right for the threat, but it was his show and Edwards had to play along. "C'mon, Jeebs, the man is crazy, he'll do it. Better give it up."

"I don't have anything, I don't *know* anything!"

"One . . ."

"Really, Kay, I swear!"

"Two . . ."

"Give it up, Jeebs," Edwards said. "That thing has got a hair trigger."

"Three."

Kay squeezed the trigger.

The *ka-boom!* was real loud as it bounced off the walls and floor and ceiling.

Jeebs's head exploded. Blood and brains flew everywhere. He dropped the toaster.

Holy shit!

Jeebs collapsed like a boneless chicken, half his head just . . . gone.

Edwards's training didn't completely desert him. Somehow, he managed to pull his own weapon. He pointed it at Kay, who'd already lowered his piece to point at the floor. "Put it down! Put it down right now!"

Scumbag or not, you couldn't just *execute* somebody like that, no matter which goddamned agency you worked for.

Not even in New York City. Hell, not even in *Brooklyn!*

Well, the Bronx or Queens, maybe . . .

"I warned him."

"Put. The. Gun. Down."

"*You* warned him, too."

"Read my lips, asshole. You are under arrest. You have the right to remain silent. If you give up that right, anything you say can and will *no doubt* be used against you in a court of law. You have the right to an attorney. If you cannot afford one—"

"Lighten up, Edwards. What you going to arrest me for? Discharging a firearm in the city limits?"

"You're crazy, you know that?" Edwards gestured at the dead man with his pistol. "Discharging a firearm, I got you discharging a firearm right here—" abruptly he shut up because the sudden short circuit in his brain stopped his mouth from working. His lips moved, but no sound came out.

He must have looked like a fish pulled onto a boat deck.

He was looking right at Jeebs when *the dead man got to his feet!*

Blap. Just like that, blown-open head and all.

Oh, *man!*

He felt his mouth gape, but he was unable to control it. His gun arm sagged until his pistol was pointed at the floor, couldn't control that, either.

Man—

Jeebs's head flowed, morphed, and re-formed into a new head.

I never even did any acid, how can I be having a flashback?

The new head looked at Kay. "I wish you wouldn't *do* that."

Kay stepped forward, grabbed Jeebs, and shoved his pistol under the rebuilt chin. "I don't have time to screw around here, Jeebs. Show me the toys or I'll use up another head. At the least."

Edwards said, "Man. No way. No way in hell."

"All right, all right," Jeebs said. "In the back."

Jeebs started toward the counter, Kay following him. Kay turned to look at Edwards. "You just gonna stand there and catch flies in your mouth?"

Edwards shook his head. Closed his mouth. Reholstered his piece. No way he was gonna try arresting anybody and try to explain this one. A guy with funny eyes and a *Star Wars* blaster was one thing; watching Jack

Jeebs get his head blown off and him acting like it was a bad haircut, that was something else again. He had no desire to spend his next few years in the loony bin, thank you. He wasn't ever gonna tell anybody about this. He followed the two.

In the back, Jeebs went to a shelf. He touched a hidden control and the shelf rotated, revealing more boxes on the other side. Any other time, this would have been a pretty neat trick, but after that exploding head, it was petty shit.

Jeebs pointed at a box. "There's the hardware."

"Come take a look," Kay said to Edwards. To Jeebs, he said, "And you stay right there. Don't you move a pseudopod."

Edwards walked over, looked in. There were a bunch of things in the box; they looked like a display from a sci-fi convention. From their shapes, Edwards guessed that most of them were weapons. He looked up. Maybe he had been right. He had a great fear that Captain Kirk or Luke Skywalker was gonna walk in the door any second now and he was not ready for that. No way. No how.

Jeebs said, "If you're interested, I can make you a nice deal on an electrostatic deoxygenator, Kay. With full zoids, no extra."

"I already got one. Shut up, Jeebs."

"There it is," Edwards said. "That one looks just like the one the guy I chased had." He pointed but did not touch the thing. He had no desire to put his hand into that box. Might get him sent into some other dimension. Weird?

Sheeit. That word didn't even belong in the same *dictionary* as whatever this mess was. His head hurt. He needed to go lie down. For a week or two. Somewhere far away from this town. Alaska, maybe. Or Staten Island.

Kay shook his head at Jeebs. "Jeebs, Jeebs. You sold a reverberating carbonizer with implosion capacity to an unlicensed, illegal cephlapoid?"

Jeebs shrugged. "He said he left his license in his other body. He looked okay to me."

"Did he now?"

"He had cash, Kay."

Kay cut his gaze at the ceiling, then back at Jeebs. "Now, you know he wouldn't have needed hardware like that unless he was buying it for a hit. Who's the target?"

"He didn't say."

Kay raised the weapon. Edwards stood there, mildly curious to see if Jeebs would grow yet another head if Kay blew this one off.

"Come on, Kay, why would he tell me that? I don't know! All I did was sell him the piece!"

Kay lowered his gun. Sighed. "All right, Jeebs. It's confiscated, all of it. And I want you on the first transport out of the gravity well—or next time I'll shoot you where it doesn't grow back."

Jeebs grinned nervously, more like a rictus than a smile. Probably thought he was getting off light. Thrown out of the gravity well.

Gravity well. Yeah, right. Whatever the hell that was.

Edwards tried to recover. "Yeah. And we're taking the Rolex fakes, too."

They walked out of the shop. Suddenly the thought of sitting down on the curb right there seemed like a great idea. He sat. He stared at the box of Rolexes. No answers in there.

Kay came out with the box of sci-fi gear, fiddled with an electronic alarm cutoff, took the stuff to the car, and put it into the trunk.

Edwards watched him. It looked like somebody had come by the Ford and dumped a bunch of ashes and dust all around it, but otherwise the car was untouched.

That the car was okay was almost as much of a surprise as Jeebs and his exploding head. This still was New York City.

Unless maybe it wasn't. Maybe any second now, ole Rod Serling holding a cigarette would step out from the pawnshop all in scratchy black and white and that doo-doo-doo-doo music would crank up behind him: "Meet James Edwards. An unremarkable cop who thought when he left for work this morning it was going to be just another day chasing criminals. James Edwards, who tripped and stumbled and when he got back to his feet, found himself no longer in New York City, but instead, in . . . the Twilight Zone."

Doobee-de-do-waahhh!

After he shut the trunk, Kay walked back over to where Edwards sat, and sat next to him.

"Having a little trouble putting a handle on it, aren't you, son? It's not exactly the kind of thing you can find a proper drawer to file it in, is it? I bet you wouldn't mind if I offered some kind of rational explanation, would you? Here, have a fake Rolex."

Edwards took the watch. Stared at it.

"Want me to give you some answers?"

"Please."

Kay lit a cigarette, took a deep drag, blew a thin stream of smoke into the already smoggy New York air. Said, "Afraid I can't help you a whole lot. You only got a leeetle sliver of the pie and look at the mess it made out

41

of your day. I mean, I *could* tell you, but you wouldn't remember it anyway. Be wasting both our time."

"Mister, no way in hell I could ever forget this. It would be the last thing on my mind as they lowered me into the grave."

Kay put on his shades, took what looked like a little tape recorder from his pocket. "You think? Here, ever see one of these, son?"

Edwards looked. What—?

There came a bright flash of light—

—light glinted off something and Kay said, "—and his wife said, 'Yeah, I know, Harry, but this one is eating my *popcorn!*'"

Kay laughed and Edwards blinked. He looked down, saw a half-eaten order of broccoli and beef and several empty bottles of Chinese beer on the table. He looked around.

Yep, a Chinese restaurant, all right, people eating, talking, laughing.

How the hell had he gotten here? And where had he gotten here *from*?

Kay glanced at his watch, a Rolex or a pretty good fake, and said, "Oops, gotta run. Thanks for the egg rolls and the help. See you tomorrow, nine A.M. sharp."

Edwards blinked again. "Where are we?"

"See what I said about too much tequila, son? You really need to moderate your drinking a little. I hope you don't get hangovers."

Kay got up, dropped some bills on the table, and left. Edwards stared at his plate. Man. He couldn't remember anything since—since—he stopped and thought about it. Since he'd left the station with this guy to go somewhere.

Where? Here? After drinking enough tequila to black out?

Hell, he hadn't gotten that plowed since he'd been in high school.

He didn't remember anything. Damn. This was . . . bad.

The waitress came over. "Another beer?"

"No ma'am. Coffee."

While he waited, he looked down again, saw a business card on the table. His name, tomorrow's date, the time—9 A.M.—and address were written on the card. The address was on Battery Drive. He turned the card over but there was nothing there except three letters centered: MiB.

He looked at his watch.

A Rolex? Or a pretty good copy of one. Where had that come from?

What did all this mean?

He shook his head. Something wasn't right here. Probably be a good idea to find out what that was.

If he got out of this alive, Kerb thought, that Bulare used-ship seller was going to pay through the sabal tube for sticking him with this piece of Garzian junk. The little twerp would be sorry his great-great-great-grandmother's egg had ever hatched. And then some.

Well, yes, to be sure, Kerb had been in a big hurry and had not really pursued his inspection. That was his fault. And true, he hadn't had a lot of scratch to spend on a ship he planned to use for just the one round trip before he junked it. But even so, that did not excuse the Bulare. *He* hadn't known that.

He sighed. They must have seen him coming a parsec away.

The sale had been criminal. The ship's warp engines were crap, the repellors were shot, the computer's viral matrices were scrambled, and,

6

and the isonic dampers were disharmonic to the third damned power. All of which meant he was going to thump down on this dung ball of a planet at speed, way, way too fast, and if the stasis cocoon couch didn't work any better than the rest of the zerksucker of a ship, he was going to be splattered all over the countryside in a damp and lumpy chitinous sheet, and so much for his grand cosmic plan.

Damn. If he got out of this alive, he was definitely going to go back and grind that seller into organic mush and feed him to himself.

If he got out of it alive.

The computer, whose sense of humor had apparently been corrupted along with the viral-molecular matrix that ran its vox program, informed him that landing was imminent: "Planetfall in fifteen seconds," it said. "Structural integrity of the outer hull is insufficient to withstand impact velocity. Hee, hee, hee. Damage estimate to vessel, approximately seventy-eight percent, plus or minus one percent. Haw, haw, haw. Hee, hee, heeee."

Kerb told the computer to chase itself, an action unlikely save for a very few races and none of them particularly bright. The computer thought this hilarious and laughed the final few seconds until the ship smashed into the ground hard enough to bury half its diameter and splash the earth up around it like liquid.

Kerb didn't see this, of course, because the stasis couch cocoon deployed and it was his great and good fortune that it was the one piece of equipment that worked as designed. On impact, the couch formed a gelatinous shell around him that absorbed most of his inertia, not incidentally making him blind, deaf, and otherwise insensate in the process.

When the couch released him—a procedure something like a krit coughing up a partially digested food ball to feed its young—it was obvious the idiot computer had been right about the hull's integrity. Night air wafted through great rents in the vessel, an atmosphere that was to him too cold and too filled with alien stinks vile enough to turn the stomach of a pluvian carrion eater.

Gah.

Something jabbered at him in an alien tongue. Kerb found his interneural universal translator button where it had fallen onto the couch, and inserted it into his aural canal. The device picked up the alien language and converted it into omniversal in mid-sentence: "—make one false move and I'll blast your outer space ass to kingdom come!"

Kerb shifted his position so he could see through one of the gaping holes in the ship's hull. Well, well. There it was. A human. Or, as they were known galacticly, a terry—they certainly were ugly, fleshy, stunted little bastards—pointing what was obviously a projectile weapon at the ship.

They never learned, these inferior species.

Kerb said, "Put the gun down, stupid."

His vox box translator, linked to the UT in his aural canal, transformed his command to "Place the projectile weapon upon the ground, less than optimal brained one."

Well, that was close enough.

The terry skittered away for an instant, then edged back into view. It leveled the weapon at the ship again. "My name is Edgar Yax and that's my pickup truck your damned spaceship just landed on and squashed! You owe me for it, pal. And as for my gun, you can have *that* when you pry it from my cold dead fingers!"

"There's a deal," Kerb said to the Edgar. That came out as, "Your proposal is acceptable."

Kerb extended one of his chela and grabbed the Edgar by the head. The Edgar went "Urk!" and fired his projectile weapon but the blast was ill aimed and did no harm, save possibly to bacterial passersby in the air.

Kerb dragged the Edgar into the ruined ship, killed it by carefully crushing the crunchy skull with his pincher, then examined the corpse.

It was so *small.* He would have to fold himself into N-space to get it on and even then, it would be a struggle. And such flimsy integument, the skeleton was internal! What a stupid design! He'd have to spit-coat the inside or it would rip like spiger lace in a stiff breeze. And even then, it would be an iffy proposition to move without tearing the damned thing every time he moved.

Always something on these dead-end planets.

He sighed. Well. One made do with what one had. The Edgar was one of the ruling species and that was that, end of story. If he wanted to move around as one of them, he had to look like one of them. No point in putting it off.

Kerb folded himself into N-space—ow! that was always so painful!—and began the most unpleasant process of shrugging himself into the former Edgar's integument.

Another of the Edgar's species, a female, stood in the entranceway to the artificial cave nearby. What did they

47

call them here? Houses? It said, "Edgar? Everything all right? You look kind of piqued."

Might as well get used to the identity. From now on, Kerb would think of himself as Edgar, at least as long as he wore the disguise. Edgar. Edgar. Edgar. All right, he had it now.

Being folded into N-space was not only painful and irritating, it also made him hungry. The ship's replicator hadn't worked worth dung the last four cycles and he was starving when he ate the remains of the Edgar. Now, after such a hasty meal, he was thirsty. He needed a nice drink.

This female was obviously the property of the Edgar, so best he treat it accordingly.

The female said, "What was that, blowed up the truck?"

"Sugar," Edgar said.

"Sugar? I never seen sugar do that before."

"Silence, you twit. Get me sugar, now!"

The female made a gesture with its shoulders and went to a nearby box made of what appeared to be some organic woody plant carved and planed into flat sheets, opened a door, and removed a container. He could smell the sweetness in it.

"Put it in water."

The female obeyed, poured a small measure into a see-through container.

"More," Edgar said. "Be not parsimonious."

The female tipped more of the white granules into the see-through container. Edgar grabbed it from her, downed it in one swallow. Ah. That hit the spot. He felt a warm glow suffuse him. Couple more of these and he'd be ready to party.

"E-E-Edgar, the skin on your neck, it's just kind of . . . hanging there. Did you get burned out at the truck?"

Edgar put the see-through container down on a platform and observed his reflection in the see-through substance that allowed observation of the outside from within the house. What was that aperture called? He queried his translator. *Window*. Right.

The female was correct. The integument had slipped a bit. He grabbed the face of it, twisted it back into place, and tucked the excess down into the opening of the clothing covering the disguise. "Better?" he said.

The female collapsed, apparently unconscious.

Hmm. How odd. Some kind of local ritual?

Well, to business. A few more helpings of the sugar and then back to the ship. He would have to move it, hide it somewhere, and repair it. Probably there was a nano-fix kit in the toolbox, so he could at least get the hull patched and some basic engine functions back online. Doubtful the ship would be able to go more than a few dozen light-years with such spugor-rigging, but that would probably be enough to get him somewhere he could get a real vessel. He'd just have to limp along as best he could.

Always something that went wrong. Never failed. The gods of chaos must get bored easily, to keep poking their pinchers into his business the way they kept doing.

He went back to the ship, dug under the rear, being careful not to tear his new integument, and lifted the ship out of the crater. He dropped it on the ground. Oof! Not so much heavy as awkward. He looked around. No other houses nearby, that was fortunate. There were empty fields and patches of tall woody-stalked plants—trees, the translator told him—even some four-legged mammalian creatures here and there, but none of the human terrans about. Good.

He briefly considered returning to the structure and eating the female, but decided against it. She looked stringy and tough, and he wasn't all that hungry anymore. He'd pick somebody up later.

He shook his head, then began pushing the ship along the ground. It was awkward, slow work. It would be much easier if he could slip the disguise off and just carry the ship on his back, but that would mean unfolding and refolding himself, then stretching the disguise on again, a prospect he did not relish in the least. Better to do it this way than have to go through *that* again.

Edgar sighed. It was always something.

James Edwards stood across the street from the building whose address matched that on the card in his hand. It was a mild day, the smog wasn't too bad, and he thought he heard a bird singing. Either that or somebody's car alarm in the distance.

During the winter, first time the snow fell and covered the city, making everything pristine white for a few moments, it looked nicer, but for New York in the summer, it was about as good as it got.

He looked at the structure. It was a squat, square building, he probably had passed it a hundred times and never noticed it before. Big deal, he'd lived in New York all his adult life and there were thousands of buildings he'd never noticed, unless a perp ran into one.

Oh, well. He tapped the card, then jaywalked

7

across the street, ignoring the cabbie who honked at him.

Inside, the place had a weird look to it. The security door was heavy steel with mesh as thick as pencils—that was normal enough—but one whole wall was dominated by huge blades of a tunnel vent-air intake. Made no sense to put that in the *lobby*. The designer must have been on drugs, place wasn't big enough to need that much air.

There was a single elevator at the far end of the room, and an old security guard sat perched on a folding metal chair halfway between the entrance and the elevator. He was reading a comic book. Talk about cheap, they couldn't even give the guy a desk?

Edwards walked toward the guard, his footsteps echoing hollowly in the mostly empty room. The old geezer looked up.

"He'p you?"

"Uh, yeah, I got this card—"

"Elevator," the guard cut in. "Push the 'call' button." He looked back down at his comic. Cackled at something funny in the book.

Edwards shook his head and walked to the elevator. Here was a no-class place. Why would this guy Kay want to meet him here?

Why would anybody want to come here at all?

As he approached the elevator, the doors *thwipped* open, just like on *Star Trek*. There was nobody inside. What the hell. He stepped inside. Hit the call button.

Nothing happened. He reached out to hit the button again.

"Ahem," somebody cleared their throat behind him.

Edwards spun. The back wall of the elevator was gone and there was another weird room in front of him. Half a dozen men sat in egg-shaped chairs, all of the guys looking at him. There was one empty chair. An old guy in a black suit, white shirt, and tie stood facing the chairs. Dressed just like Kay had been. Maybe they got a discount on the suits somewhere. Bulk rate, probably.

"You're late," the old guy said. "Have a seat."

Edwards shrugged, moved to the empty chair.

The elevator door slid shut.

The old guy nodded and said, "My name is Zed. You're here because you are the best of the best. You number among the best Navy SEALs, Army Rangers, and New York's finest."

Some of the other six men, all short-haired and straight-spined, cast glances at Edwards where he slouched in his chair.

Military dudes, all of them. He knew the look. Smug bastards. He smiled and gave it right back to them.

The old man said, "We're looking for just one of you. What will follow is a series of simple tests to quantify your motor skills, hand-eye coordination, concentration, and stamina."

Edwards raised his hand.

"Yes, you have a question, or do you need to go to the bathroom?"

"Yeah. I must have lost my notebook. Why exactly are we here?"

One of the other dudes shot his hand into the air. Oh, man. There was always one fool like him in school: I know, I know, pick me!

Zen nodded at the guy. "Son?"

The guy said, "Jake Jensen, sir! West Point, first in my class. We're here because you are looking for the best of the best of the *best*, sir!"

53

Edwards laughed. He tried to stifle it, but not too hard.

Zed looked at him like he was a dog who'd piddled on the rug. "Something funny we're missing here?"

"Best of the best of the best of the best? Sounds like a rap song." He looked around, expecting to see smiles. Didn't see any.

Oops.

Nobody was with him here. He shook his head. These military dudes were tight-assed, they had no sense of humor. Gung-ho, into the valley of death, all that shit. Stupid.

"It, ah, struck me as funny," Edwards finished.

Zed gave him another of those dog-just-peed-the-carpet looks. "Okay, let's move on."

The other six guys stood as one, like they were machines. Edwards got to his feet more leisurely. Whatever these dudes were into, he didn't think he wanted to be part of it. But he might as well go along and see where it led, given that he'd come this far.

Edwards looked at the test paper on his lap, then around at the other six men, who likewise had papers balanced on their knees, trying to write on them. This was stupid, they couldn't come up with some desks?

There was a small table against one wall. Nobody was using it. Hell with this. He got up, walked over to the table, and dragged it back in front of his little egg chair. The other testees glared at him as he moved the table. It made considerable racket scraping across the floor, but hey, that wasn't his problem. He wasn't going to be punching no holes into his good pants for some silly-ass IQ test.

And he had to say, it was pretty damned silly: "If you hold a spoon under the stream of water running from the faucet into your kitchen sink, the water will spray farthest from it: a) bowl up or: b) bowl down?"

Jesus. What kind of question was that? They must not be looking for rocket scientists here, that was for damn sure.

Edwards pondered over another silly question: Mr. White drove a train. Mr. Lee had a dog. Miss Jones did not go to Church on Sunday. Mr. Chin lived next to Mrs. McGraw. A whole bunch more crap like that, then you get to the bottom, they asked: Who owns the zebra?

There wasn't a thing in there about any damned zebra. How were you supposed to figure that out?

Who gave a rat's ass? What would they want with a zebra anyhow? He could just see trying to take a striped jackass for a walk in the park. Be big dogs chasing it, muggers trying to rip it off, plus the Baggies you'd have to carry to clean up after the damned thing would have to be garbage-can-sized. He could just see himself leading a zebra with one hand and a bag full of road apples in the other.

Who owns the zebra . . . ? Man . . .

He noticed Zed glance over toward a smoked-glass panel in one wall. Somebody on the other side of it, Edwards couldn't make out who, watching. Hell with this. This didn't get more interesting pretty quick, he was going to take a hike.

Zed herded the seven of them into another room, this one was *really* weird because it was triangular shaped. There was nothing in it but a counter and on the counter, seven handguns. Looked like SIGs, nines or forties.

What, were they going to have to field-strip the pieces?

Maybe they were going hunting for zebras. . . .

He was tempted to ask the jarhead next to him—what else could he be with that Semper Fi tattoo on his forearm?—why they were here.

Nah, he decided, no point in getting that best-of-the-best crap thrown at him again. He'd figure it out—

All of a sudden the walls just kind of . . . pulled apart. And all of a sudden, there was a shitload of stuff going on: lights flashing, sirens screaming, and all kinds of . . . things, bug-eyed monsters, ugly critters, even a little girl, all right there.

"Gentlemen, protect yourselves!" an amplified voice yelled.

Hogan's alley, Edwards realized. A shooting gallery.

The seven of them all went for the pieces. This was obviously a hand-eye-motor-skill-can-you-shoot-worth-a-crap test.

Edwards snatched up one of the pistols, checked out the horde of creatures—

Six shots went off, pretty much altogether. Damn, these guys were fast.

He picked his target and fired, nearly a second behind the other six. He pulled the trigger again, for a double-tap to make sure, but the gun clicked empty. Only one round. Interesting.

The targets froze. The lights dimmed, the sirens stopped. The six guys all looked at each other, then at Edwards. He could almost hear what they were thinking: Too slow, pal. You're history.

"Gentlemen, table your weapons, please."

Zed stepped into the room. He walked straight to Edwards. The other six tried to hold their smiles in check.

"Took your time, didn't you?"

"I needed to be sure of my target, sir."

Zed turned and looked at the targets. The most obvious in the frozen holographic crowd—and Edwards was pretty sure that's what it was, a hologram—was the big snarling beast that looked kind of like the Tasmanian Devil from the Warner Brothers cartoons. It had three holes in its chest. Next to Taz was a really ugly sucker who looked like some pissed-off god had given it a fishhook for a head. It also had three holes at the center of mass.

At the back of the horde was an eight-year-old girl. She had a single bullet hole right between her eyes.

Zed looked back at Edwards. "Mind if I ask why you felt little Tiffany back there deserved to die?"

One of the military yahoos snickered.

"Son?"

"She was the only one who seemed dangerous."

A couple more of the military guys chuckled.

"And you came to that conclusion how?"

"Well, your hookheaded guy, he can't have any brains in that thing, so they are probably in that bean bag connected to it with that umbilical there, and since he's not carrying it, he isn't coming at us. And that butt-ugly thing there, it looks like he's snarling, but what I think is, he's sneezing, that looks like Kleenex in his hand. Got to figure a guy sneezing isn't much of a threat. Besides, from his eyes, you can see he's not even looking at us.

"The little girl, well, she doesn't really look like a little girl should. The face is crooked, the stance is weird, she doesn't really look like a little girl ought to. And why

57

is she in this crowd? Nobody is holding her hostage and anybody looking for a threat would probably consider her the last target they'd shoot at."

"That's it?"

"That looks like a knife in her hand."

"What knife? I don't see a knife."

"It was there before. Either she dropped it or you made it go away."

"You saying we cheated, son?"

"I didn't say that. You did." Edwards shrugged. "Besides, there's the books."

"What about them?"

"Way too advanced for somebody her age. Look at the titles."

"You can see that?"

Zed looked at the other six men and shook his head. They mirrored his gesture.

Well, okay, so he wasn't gonna qualify first, Edwards thought. Big hairy deal. He didn't even know what he was supposed to be qualifying *for*. But he smiled along with the other six. He was going to get kicked out, he was going to look cool when it happened and unlike these gung-ho shiffs, he could do cool.

Edwards said, "So what's next, chief?" He improvised: "What be the test, for the best of the best of the best-best?"

Any fool could do bad rap, it didn't take any talent. Good rap was hard, weren't but a few could could pull that off, but even the bad stuff still found an audience. Shoot, TV could make almost anyone look good doing it these days.

Zed apparently was not a fan, from his expression. Well, too bad.

• • •

Kay stood in the hall watching the would-be recruits through the smoked glass, smiling. He hefted the thick manila folder he held as Zed came in, shaking his head. "Your boy has a real problem with authority."

"He got the right target. Your military mopes cooked a harmless Ketuvian leaf eater with a head cold and a hookhead kitten who only wanted to lick their faces," Kay offered.

"He's going to be more trouble than he's worth."

"Hell, Zed, the kid ran down a cephlapoid on *foot* and then walked away from a hand-to-hand with it. How many people we got can do that?"

"You made up your mind already, haven't you? No point in me even saying anything, is there? I hope you know what you're doing."

"I almost never do, but that never stopped me before."

"No, that's true." Zed shook his head again.

"Let's wind it down."

Kay watched as Zed rounded the corner and went back into the shooting gallery. The older man led the recruits back to the main interview room. Kay followed them. Saw Edwards see him.

"Hey, hey, it's Mister Kay. How you doing?"

Kay smiled. The kid did have a certain charm. Reminded him of himself thirty years ago. "Hold up there, sport," Kay said.

Edwards hung back a little. Zed took the other six men ahead.

"You want to know what is going on?"

The kid shrugged. "Been having so much fun, it doesn't really matter. But if it makes you happy . . ."

As they walked, Kay said, "Back in about nineteen fifty-four or fifty-five, the government started a little under-funded agency with the simple purpose of making contact with a race not of this planet. It seemed pretty funny at the time, so the government didn't exactly spread the word far and wide. The money got bled off some slush funds and only a handful of people even knew the agency existed." He tapped the folder with his free hand.

Ahead of them, Zed led the six troopers into a small alcove. "One final test, gentlemen. If you'll look right here . . ." He held up a neuralyzer.

Edwards started to move in that direction.

Kay grabbed his arm. "Where are you going?"

"Dudes getting another test, I don't want to be left out."

"Yeah, you do. This way. Look over there."

Edwards turned to look. The neuralyzer's flash strobed the wall, but the reflection wasn't enough to cause any harm, you had to be looking directly at it.

Edwards started to turn around.

"Don't bother, son, they have other things on their mind right now." He handed Edwards the folder. "Check out the pictures."

The first one was back when he was a trainee, early sixties. Nine of the team, all in their standard black suits, standing around a metal desk under fluorescent lights, pale skins, looking like Dracula's kids. God, had he ever been that young?

"Nice," Edwards said.

"Thing is, the aliens made contact, upstate New York, back in the early sixties."

Edward shuffled to the next picture. A grainy b&w of

two ships hovering in the night sky, classic flying saucer stuff.

"There were seven Men in Black then—that's what the MiB stands for, and it's as good a name as any. Plus an amateur astronomer who spotted the ship and one stupid kid who got lost on a back road on his way to pick up his date and happened to be in the wrong place at the wrong time. We all got to the ships right after they landed."

The next picture showed the ship, the hatch open, unmistakable alien shapes inside. At the portal, a very young-looking Kay stood, holding a bouquet of flowers.

"Go on. You brought flowers to the little green men?"

They moved into B corridor, impossibly long for the building in which they were in. Kay noticed, as always, the odor of spice as he entered the corridor.

Kay said, "The first ones were intergalactic refugees and they were looking for someplace apolitical, a neutral place where a few of them at a time could hang out. Kind of like Switzerland. Or maybe like Rick's place in *Casablanca*."

"I saw that movie. Pretty good."

"The powers-that-were decided to go along with it."

The next picture was a killer.

"Hey, that's the World Fair, out in Queens, right? Still under construction. We studied about it in state history. Up on those towers, are those, uh . . ."

"Yes. The flying saucers from that first meeting."

"You mean the World's Fair was a . . . cover-up for alien contact?"

"Why else would anybody have a World's Fair in Queens?"

Edwards nodded. "I hear that." He paused for a second, then said, "So you're saying the earth is like Rick's place in *Casablanca,* is that right?"

"More or less. We have a small nonhuman population now, living among us in secret."

"Do tell. Don't take offense, Mr. Kay, but when was the last time you had a CAT scan?"

"Couple of months ago. Company policy, twice a year, full-scale physical. I didn't have a brain tumor then."

"Uh-huh. So it's either drugs or some kind of psychosis, is that it? Well, thanks for the visit and all but I think maybe it's time for me to be heading on back to the precinct. The sarge'll be worried about me, you know?"

Kay shrugged as they came abreast of the kitchen. The door was closed. "If that's what you want. Lemme grab a cup of coffee here and I'll show you the way out."

He opened the door and held it for Edwards. The kid took two steps and stopped as if he'd turned to stone. Kay had to smile.

Three Vermars, tall and reedy aliens who looked a lot like man-sized centipedes balanced on their tails, stood next to a water cooler, shooting the breeze. They spoke Vermararian, which always sounded to Kay like a cross between Esperanto and microphone feedback. And they smelled like fresh doughnuts.

Iggy, the senior of the triad, waved a pseudopod at Kay as he went to get coffee.

"How they floating, Iggy? Damn, don't tell me we're out of cream again? All we got is this powdered shit?"

Iggy chittered. Pointed at the counter.

"Oh, yeah, thanks. I didn't see it." He found the cream behind a box of stale doughnuts. "Thanks, Iggy."

Kay poured some cream into his coffee, stirred it, then looked at Edwards. "Okay, kid, you ready to roll?"

Edwards stood there with his mouth open, staring. Kay nodded at the Vermars. "See you around, guys."

They gave him some feedback squeals and waved.

Kay walked to where Edwards stood. Put one finger under his chin and pushed his mouth closed. "For future reference, this is a better look for you," he said. "Besides, some of our clients take that open mouth as a threat, you know?"

Edwards looked at him.

"C'mon, kid. Let's go take a walk. I'll fill you in on what you need to know."

He took the kid out the back way; no point in rattling him any more than he already had been.

He was gonna be all right, Kay was pretty sure of it. After doing the job for thirty years, you got a feel for people. Of course, he and Dee had been partners for so long he hadn't ever had to break in a new one for himself, though he had done basic training on a bunch of the boys before shipping them off to their assignments. Some of those special forces types back there would be drooling and gibbering by now and while the kid was stunned, he wasn't afraid.

No, the young cop wasn't doing so bad, all things considered. No worse than he had done, certainly.

"This way. We want to stay on the green line this trip." He pointed at the floor.

Edwards followed him, but kept looking back behind him, like a leashed puppy who has spotted a squirrel and doesn't want to leave it behind.

James Edwards sat on the bench in Battery Park next to Kay—
—still the only name he'd been given, first or last—who sipped at his coffee. He kept trying to get his mind around it but it just didn't want to stretch. Aliens.

Son-of-a-bitching *aliens!*

Little green men from wherever. Damn.

Kay said, "At any given time, we've got around fifteen hundred aliens on-planet. Most of 'em right here in the city, but quite a few others spread around the whole world. And nearly all of them are decent folks, trying to make a living and to blend in."

Edwards had an epiphany. "Cabdrivers!"

Kay grinned around a mouthful of coffee. "Not as many as you might think." He gestured at one of the passersby: a tall, gorgeous woman in jogging clothes, tight shorts, tank top, headband, and earphones coming from a tape or mini-CD player. Her state-of-the-art running shoes probably cost a hundred and fifty bucks.

"Take that woman there—"

"I wouldn't mind," Edwards said. Then he thought about it. "Whoa? Don't tell me. She's an alien?"

"No. She's human. And she probably thinks she's pretty hip, knows what's what, but she doesn't have a clue that there are creatures from another world running around in midtown. And the thing is, she doesn't *want* to know."

Kay nodded at other people in the park. "That old man with the dog, those two women pushing baby carriages, they don't know, either. See it would wreck their worldview to know. Most people can't deal with the naked truth."

"People are smart, they could handle it."

"Wrong. A *person* can be smart, but people are dumb. Clump people together and spook them and what you get is a mob. And a mob is only as smart as the stupidest person in it."

He looked at Edwards. "Not that you're gonna have to worry about people who don't know our little secret. Thing is, if you join us, you won't have an outside life. No wife, no kids, nothing. You cut off contact with everybody you know outside the Black. In your case, it shouldn't take too long. And what you get for a prize is long hours, dangerous days, and no recognition. You don't even get a favorite shirt—unless you like white."

Edward stared at Kay. "Why would anybody in his right mind go for this deal?"

"Nobody in his right mind would, given the choice. The only satisfaction you get is doing the job, being one of a handful of people who *can* do the job."

Kay pulled another picture from the file and handed it to Edwards. It was the kid with the flowers. Definitely Kay, a whole lot younger. He faced an alien from five feet away, but the flowers were now down on the ground, scattered around his feet.

"There's the speech," Kay said. "The one I didn't get. I didn't volunteer, see, I got drafted. You get a choice."

Edwards shook his head. "I don't know."

"Smart. One of the smartest things you could say. Up until about five hundred years ago, almost everybody on the planet thought the world was flat. That if you sailed far enough away from known territory, you'd drop right over the edge and fall off, landing God knew where. But they were wrong.

"Four hundred years ago, almost everybody who knew anything knew that the world was the center of the universe. No question, the sun revolved around us, we were it. They were wrong, too.

"Two hundred years ago, the best doctors in Europe thought disease came from the aether, bad night air, and you slept with your windows closed so it wouldn't get into your house and get you.

"Fifty years ago, a good breakfast was bacon, eggs, bread, butter, milk, coffee, maybe some cereal with cream and lots of sugar. All the experts said if you wanted to stay healthy, you'd better eat like that."

"You have a point?" Edwards said.

"Yeah. A hundred years from now, whoever is here will probably pee themselves laughing at what we believe. Thing is, we don't live in the future, we live in the now. And *now*, the truth is, we have aliens walking around on our planet. Only a handful of people know this, and at the moment, you are one of them. You're like the guy who knew the the world was round when nobody else believed it. The guy who knew germs caused disease, that the earth wasn't the center of the universe, that bacon and eggs will clog up your arteries and kill you deader than black plastic. You have access to a piece of the truth that most people don't. The truth isn't always popular or pretty, but it is the truth."

Edwards stared out into the park. "And you want me to give up my identity, never get close to anyone except—no offense—you and some other dudes in black suits? To pay for knowing the truth?"

Kay stood. He nodded. "That's the deal. Doesn't seem worth it, does it? But there it is."

Edwards looked at him.

Kay pulled something from his pocket. Looked like a mini tape recorder. He tapped it on his palm. "Tell you what. You have until tomorrow to decide."

"And if I decide not to? What is to keep me from blabbing all this to anybody I run into? Maybe taking out an ad in the paper?"

"Aside from the risk of spending the rest of your days in the lock ward of the nearest mental institution? You think anybody would believe you if you told them?"

Edwards shook his head. "Point taken."

"You wouldn't tell them, though."

"You can't be sure of that."

"Oh, I think I can." He looked at the mini tape recorder, then put it back into his coat pocket. "Be at the building tomorrow morning to let me know what you decide."

Edwards walked through the streets of his neighborhood, considering his future. It wasn't a bad part of town, relatively speaking; he seldom got awakened by gunshots and he'd learned how to tune out the sirens. A couple of the neighbors in his apartment building usually nodded or smiled at him, though that was probably because they knew he was a cop. Even his landlady sometimes cut him some slack because he was on the job—it didn't hurt to have one of New York's finest living in the building if a tenant got rowdy or some kid was casing the place to rip somebody off. Seeing Edwards come out in uniform—in the bag, plainclothes cops called it—had a certain spook value.

There was a decent bodega half a block away from his place, had great burritos and not bad ham and cheese sandwiches. Days he didn't feel like cooking—and that was most days—he could pick up something to eat there and not worry about the quality.

And Edward's place was rent controlled, too.

What more could you ask for?

He passed a wino hunched in a doorway, nodding out. Guy smelled of pee and old Mad Dog, a heavy dose of unwashed body odor thrown in.

Or—was it a wino? Maybe it was somebody from Beta Alpha VII or somewhere? Until today, he'd never considered such a thing. That sci-fi stuff, yeah, it was entertaining and all, but he never thought it affected real life.

Turned out he was wrong. He really didn't like that, being wrong.

If he stopped and shook the wino down, would he find a blaster tucked away somewhere? Some kind of futuristic thingamajig that brought in a TV signal from beyond the moon? A tentacle instead of an arm?

That's what really nagged him. Sure, he had a pretty good life, overall. True, the job was filled with dead wood, guys who were better suited to sitting in a toll booth than chasing down perps, but they weren't really his problem. Sooner or later, he'd make detective, get his gold shield, and the dead wood was part of the reason. Sooner or later, a diamond surrounded by a sea of mud is gonna get noticed.

Well, if the mud didn't keep shifting to cover the gem every time it saw daylight. Patronage had long been a part of any bureaucracy in New York and the cops were as bureaucratic as anybody. Anything above the rank of captain was suspect and a bunch of them were, too, in his experience. They might keep him down for a long time, but he was sure he could learn how to play the system. It was a game, and he rarely lost at games.

So, yeah, he could stay on the job and if he toned his attitude down and kissed a little butt now and then, he'd move up. He was smart enough to know he was smart enough to do that.

In the meanwhile, he'd be on the streets, hassling pimps, chasing dope dealers, busting hookers, shoplifters, small-time con men, muggers, rapists, and the other low-life scum who infested civilization. Somebody had to do it. And it was worth doing, no question. And, truth be told, fun most of the time.

Thing was, Edwards kind of felt like a guy who'd been issued a dip net and sent to clear minnows out of a reservoir. Nothing wrong with that—unless you looked up one day and saw a couple of sharks glide past.

How could you concentrate on minnows once you knew about the bigger game swimming around?

So, here was the question: Stay where he was, doing what he knew how to do, and do pretty damn well? Or chuck it all to join up with some quasi-secret organization full of bad dressers to deal with aliens—and not talking somebody just sneaked in on the cargo boat from some third-world country, but real, honest-to-God outer space creatures?

What's it gonna be, James?

Edgar finally found what he thought might be a hiding place for his ship, a mostly empty structure that was home to myriad small creatures, six- and eight-legged ones. From their forms, he could recognize a certain ancestral kinship. Little brothers, as it were. Or maybe little great-great-grandfathers.

Edgar was behind this structure with his ship, pondering the best way to go about getting the now-repaired vessel into the artificial cave when he heard a terran vehicle arrive and pull to a stop. He walked around the structure, saw a terry open a large door to the building, admitting inside a blast of bright sunshine. The terry was dressed in some kind of uniform. An ID tag on the creature's chest read Zap-Em. Edgar's translator couldn't turn the name into anything in Edgar's language. The Zap-Em terry carried a metal tank.

Apparently the terry did not see him, but it did notice the small creatures scurrying about inside the building, trying to hide from the light.

"Well, well, looky here," the Zap-Em terry said. He set the metal tank down and unfurled a thin hose from it. He put some kind of breathing mask over his face. He turned a valve on the tank. A vapor spewed from a nozzle on the end of the tank. The terry began to spray the substance into the building. Edgar sniffed at wisps of the escaping spew. Not a bad scent, rather invigorating, actually, compared to the bland nitrogen-oxygen-and-a few-trace-elements atmosphere. However, the gas seemed to have a deleterious effect on the scuttling small ones. They began falling over. Some kind of intoxicant?

Some kind of *poison?*

"What do you think you're doing?" Edgar asked.

The terry started, then turned to look at Edgar. "Oh, hi. I'm just taking care of your pest problem." He waved the nozzle at the small ones. "They're gonna be history in a few minutes."

Really, this was too much. He was *killing* the little brothers. Edgar said, "Pest problem. Yes, I had noticed. This planet is filled with undeveloped, unevolved, murderous pond scum. Scurrying about their short, pointless lives as though they *meant* something."

The Zap-Em terry said, "Well, yeah. Don't you want to get rid of them?"

"Oh, indeed. In the worst way." With that, Edgar grabbed the creature's breathing mask, ripped it off, then shoved the nozzle of the spraying device into the terry's oral cavity.

The Zap-Em terry choked, gagged, then fell to the ground. It gargled a few times, twitched and spasmed, then died. During its death throes, the terry dropped a metal ring with small, jagged metal bars upon it.

Edgar queried his translator. Keys. Devices for opening locks. Such as houses and vehicles. Ah.

He looked at the vehicle in which the terry had arrived. It was quite large, the vehicle. The rear section of it had sufficient room so that a careful placement of Edgar's ship would not overload it.

Aha! Here was a solution to the awkward method of moving the ship. Why leave it here when he could take it with him?

There must be something around here he could use

for a ramp. Edgar walked into the structure, to search for such a thing. He nodded at the bodies of the little brothers. "I have avenged you," he said. "And cross the Bridge in the knowledge that this terry is but the beginning."

Edward saw the old guard from the day before, sitting in the same chair, reading what looked like the same comic book. Was he something other than he appeared to be?

The guard looked up, nodded. A second later, the elevator opened and Kay stood there looking at Edwards. He raised an eyebrow.

Edwards took a deep breath, blew part of it out, nodded. "I'm in," he said.

Kay grinned. Edwards saw him put that little tape recorder into his pocket.

"This way," Kay said.

Edwards got onto the elevator, wondering how the guard had summoned Kay.

This time, the elevator began to descend when Kay touched a control.

"One thing," Edwards said. "I'm in because I don't want to be one of the sheep walking around staring at the ground. But before you beam me up to the mother ship, a couple of things I want to get straight. You chose me for my skills, but as of now, you can cease with all that 'son' or 'kid' or 'sport' shit, is that cool?"

"Cool, Slick," Kay said. "But as to all those skills of yours—"

The elevator stopped and the door slid open.

"—well, as of now, they don't mean a whole hell of a lot."

Edwards stared. The elevator had opened onto a

huge, multileveled atrium, kind of sixties in design, sleek, uncluttered, manned by humans and aliens. There was a kind of platform right outside that looked out over the giant space. Man.

An alien unlike any he'd ever seen before, walked past.

On the ceiling.

How did he? she? it? do that?

He—she—it, whatever, nodded from its upside-down walk at Kay. Made a noise halfway between a parakeet's cheep and a whoopie cushion. Kay waved at the alien. "Yeah, this is the new recruit. I'll introduce you later. Come on, son—ah, Slick."

Kay led him down a spiral ramp. They passed what looked like immigration control at the JFK airport. A human sat at a desk, a line of aliens, all kinds of aliens, stood there, waiting to be processed. A large humanoid creature stood at the front of the line, and while Edwards wasn't sure, he thought the guy looked pissed. Edwards slowed way down to check it out.

The human at the desk looked at a weird little booklet the alien tendered. Passport, had to be.

"Welcome to Earth, sir," the human said. "Purpose of your trip?"

The alien said, "Diplomatic mission."

"Length of stay?"

"Lunch."

"Anything to declare? Are you carrying any fruits or vegetables?"

Kay grabbed Edwards by the arm and moved him along. "Come on. That's an Arquillian, they tend to get a little grouchy when they're tired. Waiting in line after a seventeen-light-year flight tends to irritate almost anybody, but Arquillian transports—that's the human disguise, to you—get sneezy when they get upset and let me tell you, you do not want one of them to sneeze on you."

Edwards looked at him.

"Ever get Super Glue on your fingers?"

"Yeah."

"Imagine about a quart of it sprayed all over your face."

"I heard that. Lead on."

Kay led him away from the immigration man.

"So, now that I'm in, what branch of the government *do* we report to?"

"None, actually. Somewhere along the way, the government started asking too many questions. So we let them think we disbanded."

"Who pays for all this?" He waved at the immense center.

"Well, actually, we do. We hold a few patents on gadgets we confiscated from some of our visitors trying to smuggle them in. Velcro. Microwave ovens. Liposuction." Kay grinned. "You're gonna sprain your neck shaking your head that way. Over here."

He led him to a locked door. A light beam played over Kay, then the door clicked open. "Body reader," he said.

Inside the room were all kinds of high-tech-looking devices, stacked on tables and shelves. Kay waved one hand at them. "Amazing what people try to smuggle in. Check this out." He picked a shiny chrome device the size and shape of a matchbox with rounded corners. "Music player. Uses something like a steel marble. Got ten times the fidelity of a CD. Gonna have to buy the *White Album* again.

"Or here." He held up a metal tube and clip that looked like a lapel mike. "Universal translator. Will translate any of its programmed languages, terran or alien, into whatever other language you set it for. Guy talks to you in Chinese or Arabic or Bindooli and you hear it as English, couple of microseconds' delay is all. Useful until you learn the various languages."

Edwards stopped himself from shaking his head again.

"We're not supposed to have this," Kay said, waving the translator. "Human thought and speech are considered so primitive among the higher races they think of them as infectious diseases. Don't want to expose their children to them. Kind of makes you proud, doesn't it?"

Edwards picked up a small yellow ball. "What's this?"

"Don't touch that—!"

The ball zipped out of his hand and shot out through the door into the hallway.

"Shit—!" Kay ran out after the ball, Edwards right on his heels.

The little yellow ball zinged here and there, bounced from the walls, almost faster than the eye could follow. Humans and aliens dodged it, cursed, ducked, cursed some more.

Kay slipped an odd-looking metal glove onto his right hand, held it up. The ball bounced its way at them. Edwards ducked away but Kay reached up and caught the ball in the metal-gloved hand.

"Sorry!" he yelled. He went back into the storeroom. Put the ball carefully onto the shelf. "You remember the blackout of seventy-seven, when you were a kid?" He nodded at the yellow ball. "Practical joke by the Great Attractor. He thought it was funny as hell."

Edwards stared at him. "This your way of telling me I got a lot to learn?"

"Well, you are smarter than you look. Course, you'd have to be. Come on."

They went.

Kay led Edwards onto the main floor, where a giant video screen hung on a wall like a billboard. A pair of aliens sat at a control console in front of it. They were small, bony creatures, each with eight arms and a single eye atop a central stalk. They waved at Kay, two or three arms apiece.

"Meet the twins," Kay said. "We can't pronounce their real names but we call them Mickie and Maude. Girls, this here is the new recruit."

The twins made noises like leaky tire valves.

Edwards nodded. "How's it goin'?"

Kay turned back to look at the video.

"Flat screen," he said. "You can roll it up like a poster and put it anywhere you want. Another little gift from a smuggler. Useful, since observation is at the heart of our little endeavor."

Edwards looked at the screen. Upon it was a

9

map of the world, thousands of tiny lights flashing upon it, and log lines next to the blinking dots.

On a nearby wall, was a mural. The New York World's Fair.

Kay pulled his attention back to the screen. "This map shows the location of every registered alien on the planet. Places like New York City, you have to go to a detailed view to see them all, but we got 'em."

Kay nodded at the screen. "Most of them, a dot on the map is all we need. Some of them, we keep under closer surveillance."

Kay said, "Girls, you want to bring up the rogues' gallery, please?"

The two aliens laid hands—tentacles, whatever—on the keyboard. The map changed to hundreds of small boxes, each with a small video image. "These are the aliens. In public—what you see here—they all look human. In private, they relax a little."

Edwards stared at the screen. There was an image of a pop rock star who'd sold millions of records. Well, that wasn't any big surprise, a lot of people figured he wasn't altogether human, the way his face kept changing; but there was the guy who hosted that late-night network news TV program; there, that tall dude who did infomercials where he guaranteed to make you rich and happy. How about that?

"Doesn't make sense, does it?"

"No, no, I gotta say, it does make a kind of weird sense. I mean, when I was a third-grader, the other kids told me I was crazy because I said our teacher was from, like, Venus."

"Mrs. Edelson," Kay said.

Edwards turned to stare at him. "You're shittin' me."

Kay said, "Girls?"

A woman appeared on the screen. She had a mean face, cat's-eye glasses, and from this angle, a tail.

"Not Venus," Kay said. "Titan. One of the big moons of Jupiter, actually."

"Son-of-a-bitch."

Edwards looked up, saw Zed approaching. The older man shook his head.

"Follow me."

Edwards did as he was told. Kay was right behind him, grinning.

"Am I missing the joke?" Edwards said as they walked.

"Not really. Things have changed a little since I came onboard, but the process is remarkably similar. It is educational."

Zed led them down a corridor, around a couple of turnings, up a ramp, down a circular staircase, through a long hallway. Edwards was pretty sure he could find his way back to the main room but he wouldn't bet his neck on it. After what seemed like a walk way, way too long for them to still be in one building, they arrived at . . .

A locker room?

It was all in white: walls, ceilings, floor, lockers, benches, showers, white as a stadium full of marshmallows.

Zed led them inside. He opened a locker. Inside was a black suit on a hanger, a white shirt, and black tie. On the shelf above it, a black hat and black sunglasses, and black shiny shoes on the bottom shelf.

Your basic wardrobe in your basic colors. Dull. In the extreme. Could put a speed junkie to sleep just looking at it.

"From now on, you'll dress in sanctioned attire, supplied to you by MiB Special Services."

"You issue underwear too?"

Kay grinned, reached into the locker and pulled a plastic bag from under the hat. Inside the bag were black bikini briefs. "We enjoy *some* leeway. You get a choice of jockey or boxers," Kays said. "I figured you for a jock."

Edwards took the package of underwear. Shook his head and waved at the locker. "How you know this . . . stuff is gonna fit?"

"It'll fit. We got your measurements the first time you walked into the building. You dress to the left, don't you?"

"Damn, man."

"Come on," Zed said. "This is the easy part."

Edwards tossed the underwear back into the locker and closed it. "No lock. I guess nobody would steal any of this anyhow."

Kay and Zed both grinned.

Kay grinned again at the big screen in the computer room. All of Edward's ID paper was up: birth certificate, school records, driver's license, social security card, library card, police ID, everything.

Behind him, Zed said to the kid, "You'll conform to the identity we give you. You eat where we tell you, live where we tell you, *and* you get approval for any expenditure over a hundred dollars. In writing. In triplicate."

The kid gave Zed a dark look.

Kay touched a control. Behind him, Edwards said, "What's this?"

Zed said, "Have a seat. Put your hands there."

Kay turned, watched the kid slip his hands into the imprinter. The device was a flat black plate that looked as if somebody had pressed his hands into the plastic like it was soft clay, leaving deep impressions.

"Hold still, this might sting a little."

There came a burst of laser light, bright enough to seep past the kid's hands.

"Ouch! Ow!" He jerked his hands up and looked at the palms. A little residual smoke drifted from them.

"You now have a new set of fingerprints," Zed said. "They aren't on record anywhere except right here. If something happens on the job and you leave prints behind where you shouldn't, they will be changed again, so you want to be careful because it does sting a bit."

Edwards looked at his hands. "Stings. Don't be doing anything to me that *hurts,* if this is what you think *stings.* Damn, lookit that, you shortened my lifeline."

"That's not all. Don't be surprised next time you go to take a leak."

"What?!"

"Just a joke. We aren't humorless, you know. Come on, over here," Kay said.

The kid moved to look at the screen. "Hey, there I am."

"Nope. There you *were.*" Kay tapped a control. The ID onscreen whirled and vanished. What replaced it was the kid's name:

James Darrel Edwards III.

Kay said, "You just quit the force, paid your rent and gave up your lease—"

"Man, that's a *rent-controlled* apartment!"

"—you don't exist at the DMV any more, you never got a library card, a passport, or a season ticket to see the Yankees. Your credit card records went away, and your schools have no official records of you ever attending them."

"You can do that?"

"Already done," Kay said.

Zed said, "Your new image is being crafted so you don't stand out."

"I dunno, up in Harlem, that suit might make me look like a Muslim. Fit right in with Brother Farrakan and the Fruit of Islam."

Zed ignored him and continued: "You won't leave much of an impression in anybody's memory. What they probably will recall, if anything, will *be* the suit."

"I hear that. Black suit picks up everything but money and women," the kid said.

Kay grinned. "Watch." He touched a control. The name onscreen started to change as the cursor went from the right to left, backspacing and deleting:

James Darrel Edwards III

James Darrel Edw

James Darr

James

Jam

J

When it got to the final letter in the kid's name—the kid's former name—the cursor stopped.

Zed said, "As of this moment, you don't exist. You were never born. You're a rumor, a shadow, a ghost."

The kid stared at the screen. He frowned.

"You aren't part of the system. You are over it, above it, beyond it. We are 'them,' we are the 'they' people talk about in whispers. We're the Men in Black and you just became one of us. There is no James Darrel Edwards III any more. Your name from now on is Jay."

82

Kay turned away from the J onscreen and gave the kid a smile. "Welcome aboard, Jay. Now, go get dressed and let's go make the world safer."

When Edwards—no, he had to think of himself as Jay, now—came out of the locker room, Kay was waiting in the hall.

Jay touched his tie, slipped the shades on, and smiled at Kay. "See, the difference between you and me? I can pull this off. I look good. *You* look like one of the Blues Brothers with a hangover."

Kay shook his head. "A vision of sartorial splendor, all right."

"That's me. Let's rock and roll."

Jay followed Kay down another hallway. This place was huge, it had to occupy half the block, at least. And weird as it all was, it was also exciting, he had to give it that. Who'd have ever thought it? Aliens. And him joining the border patrol to keep the suckers in line.

Well. Probably not that much different from NYPD, come to think of it.

He looked at the older man walking in front of him and wondered for a second what Kay's name had been before they chopped it down. Kerry? Karl? Krebs?

Something—somebody brushed past him, but when he turned to look, all he saw was what looked like a kind of ghostly trail, like motion images on a time-exposed photograph. Wasn't anybody connected to them.

He started to say something, then changed his mind. He was gonna be asking a lot of questions and that got old quick. He'd just go along and see what got volunteered. After all, he was one of the team now, and it had to be better than the team where he'd played last, right?

. . .

Edgar piloted the Zap-Em ground vehicle toward Manhattan. His current location was a place called New Jersey. The piloting—driving they called it here—had become increasingly precarious. The number and varieties of vehicles upon the paved paths he had been following—called variously, for reasons he could not determine, road, street, avenue, place, way, highway, tollway, boulevard, lane, promenade—had increased steadily, so that now, he was forced to creep along at a speed a Wiverian blood-slug could match, or even better, if it was feeling frisky.

How *did* these creatures manage to build a civilization if they couldn't construct vehicle pathways sufficient to allow free movement? As with so many other things about this mudhole of a planet, this made no sense. Any sentient being with two neurons to rub together knew that if the path was too narrow, you flattened whatever was to the sides and widened the path until the flow of vehicular traffic was unimpeded. It was a basic tenet. This . . . bottleneck effect was idiocy to the fifth power.

At least they could have equipped these wheeled ground sloths with flight capabilites. But, no.

And one would think that any species worth dergdung would have developed a power source other than fossil fuels. Didn't they realize that such propellants were exceedingly finite? And that when they ran out of them—which they would certainly do within a short period of time if left alone—their whole species would be practically immobile?

Edgar had yet to see a solar sail, a rhemdod generator, or even a fusion bike. When the fossils got used up, they would have these useless vehicles parked everywhere, rusting away as the caustic oxygen atmosphere ate them, good for nothing save perhaps food for any passing bleemoth metal eaters who might happen to be hungry. Real hungry, given all the bleemoths would have to choose from—

A vehicle to his rear emitted a jarring blast of noise. This was, Edgar had learned from experimenting with the steering controls of his own vehicle, a warning device. A horn, it was called, according to the translator, though the basic definition of such a thing had to do with headgear on certain large mammalian animals. The connection between that and this blare of sound produced when one pressed on the control was not apparent to Edgar.

From watching the other pilots, Edgar had learned the proper response to such a signal. He leaned the upper section of his disguise out through the open window, extended the middle digit of his port hand upward, and yelled at the pilot to his rear: "Hey, up yours, pal!"

Satisfied that he was communicating properly with these stupid terrans, Edgar leaned back to the vehicle's cockpit and concentrated on his piloting.

How did they manage it? If this was a daily occurrence, this crawl to get anywhere, surely most of them would have gone insane by now and begun killing each other?

Destroying them would be doing them a favor.

Really, it would.

Jay followed Kay into Zed's office. Zed. Wonder what *he'd* been before? Zachary? Zebadiah? Zorro?

The office was an elevated circular room with several windows, high above the main floor of the MiB HQ. There were a handful of video monitors behind Zed's desk. Each of these monitors had upon it an image of a different man, dressed as all the MiB were, along with the name of a city and a clock running the local time. Zeb sat with his back to the door, looking at the monitors, fiddling with some papers on his lap.

"We're heeerrre," Kay said.

Zed didn't look at them. "Have a seat and let me put out a few brush fires."

Jay sat, in a chair that felt a lot more comfortable than it looked, and Kay took the chair next to his. All of a sudden, there was a guy

10

standing there. And behind him, that trail Jay had noticed earlier.

He was *not* gonna ask.

The guy put a cup of coffee on the desk next to Zed. Looked at Jay. Said, "Oh, hi. Congratulations. I'm Dave."

The guy just . . . blurred, left that series of ghostly images behind him, and was gone.

Zed said, "Dave?"

Dave blurred in again. "Yes?"

"Would you get me a cup of coffee? And this is Jay, it's his first day."

Dave smiled. "Looking forward to it."

And zip, Dave was gone again.

"Hell of an assistant," Zed said, reaching for his coffee. "He does some kind of time-shift thing. Sometimes gets here before you call him. You have to remember to ask for what you wanted, otherwise, you won't have had it."

Jay stared at him. "I suppose that will make sense later."

"Not really," Zed said. "But you'll get used to it."

Jay managed to keep from saying anything stupid. He thought that was fairly good, under the circumstances.

Zed spoke to one of the monitors. "Okay, Bee, we got the recently deposed surprefect of Sinalee scheduled to touch down in the Willamette National Forest near Portland, Oregon, at twenty-two hundred tonight. I'm pulling you down from that surveillance in Anchorage for a meet and greet."

The image of Bee nodded. "Copy that. We talking humanoid?"

Zed said, "You wish. Bring a sponge." He shuffled

through the papers on his lap. Came up with a sheet and looked at it. "All right, a general memo here. Henceforth, we gotta keep Rolling Fish-Goat out of the sewer systems. He's scaring the rats and they are going places they ought not to go. Who wants that one?"

There was a loud silence.

"Fine, that one's yours, Cee."

One of the men on the monitors said, "Hey, wait a minute, why me? I had to chase Turkotte the Snot through the Namibian waste reclamation plant last week!"

"And you did such good job of it we had to shut the plant down and back up half a million gallons of raw sewage into every working toilet in the country."

"All three of them," Kay said.

"So you stop Rolling Fish-Goat and we'll call it even."

Zed came up with another memo. "Says here that Bobo the Squat wants to reveal himself on *Unsolved Mysteries*."

"I heard that was *Hard Copy*," one of the men said.

"Whatever. See that Bobo changes his mind, Tee."

"Ten-four," Tee said.

Another shuffle. A memo outlined in red. "All right, here's a red letter from last night. We had an unauthorized landing in upstate New York, farm country." He turned and looked at Kay. "That's yours, Kay. Keep your ear to the ground, we're not hosting a galactic kegger here."

Kay nodded.

"All right, go to work, people."

The screens cleared and as they did, there was a bleep! from Zed's computer. "Well, well. Got us a skimmer."

Kay leaned over and said to Jay, "That's a resident

alien traveling out of his assigned zone without permission." To Zed, Kay said, "Who is it?"

Zed looked at the screen. "Redgick."

Kay looked at Jay again. "Hmm. See, Redgick is a New Yorker, not cleared to travel outside of the city."

"Right now," Zed said, "our Mr. Redgick is way out of town. Apparently stuck in traffic on the New Jersey Turnpike. Why don't you take Jay here and show him how we do things?"

Kay nodded. "Let's go, Jay."

Outside the MiB building, the sun was shining brightly and the city had a sense of unreality about it. Given what he'd just seen inside, it should have felt normal, but somehow, it didn't.

He had to wonder if anything was ever going to feel normal again.

Jay shook his head. "What's up with the old man? Kinda hardnosed, isn't he? 'Not running a galactic kegger'? What kind of crap is that?"

"Zed was saving the world before your father was born. He's entitled to a little respect."

Jay raised his hands, held them toward Kay in a halt gesture. "Hey, I'm cool with that. Just checking."

Kay led him to the black LTD.

Jay smirked. Said, "All this galactic technology we got access to and we gonna cruise around in *this* sucker again?"

That got him a glare from Kay.

"Sorry. I'm dissing your ride again. It's a . . . nice car." He reached for the handle.

"Hold it," Kay said. "You don't want to touch it until I shut the alarm off."

"What, you think I'm gonna pee my issue drawers 'cause of a siren? I heard car alarms before."

"Not like this one, you haven't. You don't ever want to touch the car before you shut the alarm off. Remember that. It's very important."

"Man—"

"Just humor me here, okay?"

"Fine."

Inside the car, Kay started the engine. It ran quiet, had to give it that.

"Seat belt," Kay said.

"You know, you need to learn how to talk to people. You could be a little kinder and gentler, you know, like, 'Say, Jay, would you mind buckling your seat belt, please?"

Kay gritted his teeth. "Say, Jay, would you mind buckling your seat belt, please?"

"Now, see, did that hurt? Actually, Kay, my man, I prefer a bit more mobility and I find seat belts awfully restricting, so if you don't mind, I believe I'll just leave it off."

Kay smiled. Put the LTD into reverse and stomped the gas pedal.

The acceleration was unreal. Jay was thrown forward so fast he couldn't believe it. He hit the dash, bounced off the windshield, and was on the way back toward the seat when Kay shifted gears and stomped it again. The forward acceleration shoved Jay back into the seat like a fighter pilot doing a power loop. He couldn't move.

"Damn, man, how many horses you got under that hood?" Jay finally managed after half a block.

"More than enough."

"I hear you," Jay said. "Hang on a second." He grabbed the seat belt in a hurry.

As he slid the belt into the clamp, a small lighted panel rotated up between the two men, kind of like an armrest. There was a flashing red button on the panel. Jay looked at it. Put one hand tentatively toward it.

"Jay?"

"Yeah?"

"You see that red button?"

"Yeah."

"Never push the button. Under the wrong circumstances, that would be . . . how shall I say this? . . . bad."

Jay jerked his hand back.

Kay drove the big Ford with an ease that came from years of practice. Since he had a tracker, he was able to home in on Redgick's car, although he was in the middle of Nowhere, New Jersey—now there was a redundancy—when he finally caught up with the alien. He hit the siren and flashed the police lights hidden under the grill. Redgick's car pulled over.

Kay looked at the kid.

"Stay on the passenger side of his car while I check him out."

"Got it. We're, uh, not going to need weapons here, are we? I didn't find one in my locker."

"Nah, not with Redgick. He's harmless."

Kay got out of the Ford and walked to Redgick's window. He was as innocuous looking a human as he was an alien, looked to be in his mid-thirties, bland, vanilla-wafer kind of guy. Kay smiled at him. "Could I see your license and registration, please?"

Kay glanced past Redgick and saw a pregnant woman in her thirties in the passenger seat. Also in her mid-thirties, and aside from the bulging belly, unremarkable in appearance. That would be Mrs. Redgick.

The man passed him a New York driver's licence and the car's registration. Kay glanced at them. "The *other* license and registration, please."

Redgick passed a more colorful set of ID out of the car. These had holograms and watermarks and shimmery insets into the plastic. The Resident Alien cards showed Redgick and his missus in their natural form, friendly-looking, tentacled, squidlike aliens with long, thin tongues dangling, smiling at the camera. He checked the address and the verification dot with his reader, then passed them back.

"Your IDs are in order, but according to our records, you are restricted to the five boroughs unless you have a visa, which I show no record of having been issued. Am I in error here?"

"It—It's my wife. She—She—She's, well, *look!*"

As if on cue, Mrs. Redgick moaned and clutched at her belly.

Oh, shit.

Kay did not like delivering babies, especially alien babies. It was not a racial thing, just a matter of the mechanics. Some of them were real corkers. Or *un*corkers, as the case might be.

"How soon are we talking about here?"

Mrs. Redgick screamed in pain.

Soon, Kay figured. Shit.

He said, "Okay, all right, no problem, we'll handle it." He looked over the top of the car at Jay. "You handle it."

"Me?"

"Step out of the car, Mr. Redgick, and let's you and me have a little chat, while my partner helps your wife."

Redgick opened the door, looked at his wife nervously. He whispered, "Are you sure he knows what he's doing?"

"Ah, sure, he does this all the time. No problem. C'mon."

Jay stared at the woman/alien, his eyes wide.

Redgick said louder, "It's all right, sweetbug, the terran is an expert, practically a professional midwife, isn't that right?"

Kay smiled. "It surely is."

Jay leaned in, said, "Uh, hi. I'm uh, Jay."

The woman jerked her dress up over her knees and spread her legs, then moaned. That was all Kay needed to see. He led Redgick to the rear of the car.

Once there, he said, "Last I heard, Croagg the Midwife's shop was still at Sixty-fourth and Eighth, that's who you'd normally use for a delivery, isn't that right?"

"Uh, yes."

"Then why were you heading out of town?"

"I—We, ah, were supposed to meet somebody."

"Kay!" Jay screamed.

Kay glanced over that way. He couldn't see Mrs. Redgick clearly, but he did see a thin tentacle shoot up from between her knees. The tentacle waved for a second, then wrapped itself around the door post. The metal groaned.

Normal delivery, so far. Kay turned back to Redgick. "This your first?"

"Oh, no, we've got our first dozen. We sent them to visit their grandsire on the homeworld."

"Okay, so back to the question. Where were you going, exactly?"

"Uh, to catch a ship."

"Really? I didn't see a departure clearance for the

Jersey Station for today. Or for you to be on it if it was departing."

"It was the Pennsylvania Station."

"You were driving all the way to Pittsburgh?"

"It's, uh, a family emergency," Redgick offered. "On the homeworld."

"Aiiee!" Jay screamed.

Kay looked. A second tentacle had emerged from Mrs. Redgick's birth canal. This one had wrapped itself around Jay's neck. His eyes started to bulge.

"Sweet Elvis!"

"You're doing just fine, Ace." Kay looked back at Redgick. "So tell me, sport, why the sudden hurry to depart our fair planet?"

"Help! Help!"

"Some of the . . . new arrivals," Redgick offered lamely. "The neighborhood is getting so bad."

"What new arrivals are we talking about here? I don't recall letting a bunch of riffraff in lately."

"Kay, *help!*"

Kay looked again, saw Jay get one foot on the doorframe, lean back, and shove. There was a cork-from-a-wine-bottle *pop!* and he fell backward. Kay started that way, saw Jay lying flat on his back on the side of the road, the newborn baby alien square in the middle of his chest.

"Oh, man!" Jay said. The baby was looking right into his face.

Kay slapped the alien's father on the back. "Congratulations, Reggie—it's a . . . squid."

The baby cooed and gurgled at Jay, who sat up, holding it to his chest. "Hey, you know, he's a cute little—"

The alien baby puked, spraying Jay's face with greenish vomit, which effectively ended that compliment.

• • •

Back in the car, Jay wiped the last of the baby's puke off his face with a towel. "Nobody told me about this part."

"All in a day's work."

"So what's the drill here?"

"Well, I could have written Redgick a ticket for being out of his assigned area but what kind of man would do that to a couple just had a baby? Besides, they're leaving town."

"So we just let them go?"

"Ain't our job to keep them here if they want to depart the planet. Even if it's an unscheduled trip."

Jay wiped the last of the stuff from his face, and tossed the towel on the floor.

Kay sighed and shook his head. "So, what about that incident seemed unusual to you?"

Jay stared at him. "What, aside from almost being throttled by a little tentacled newborn alien?"

"Yeah."

"Why, nothing. Nothing at all. Was there something I missed?"

Kay nodded. "I guess I haven't had time to fill you in on interstellar travel. Given the vast distances between solar systems, it wouldn't be practical without the warp drive."

"Like on *Star Trek*," Jay said. "I got it."

"Something like that. Thing is, real warp travel is okay, once you get going, but it is kind of uncomfortable going in and coming out of hyperspace. Not recommended for pregnant females or newborns."

"Kind of like hot tubs," Jay offered.

Kay ignored this last offering. "So the question is, what scared Redgick so bad he'd risk a warp jump with a pregnant wife or a newborn baby? Not to mention a drive to Pittsburgh. That's more dangerous than the warp."

Jay didn't have an answer, nor did Kay really expect one.

"Maybe we better check the hotsheets and see if we can find something," Kay said.

"Can I change my clothes first?"

"Why? You don't smell bad. In fact, it smells kind of like Old Spice."

"Stuff my *father* used," Jay said.

"I use it," Kay said.

That ended that conversation, too.

Jay said, "What are we doing *here?* I thought we were going to look at the hotsheets."

Kay ignored him. Something he seemed to do a lot.

They were at one of the larger midtown newsstands. Not only had Kay gotten them there without once getting gridlocked, he'd found a parking place right in front of the stand, blap, empty, big as you please. The man must have his own personal god, to get that kind of luck. You'd be more likely to win the lottery than find an empty legal spot against the curb in this part of New York City at this time of day.

Finally, Kay said, "Follow me and learn, grasshopper."

He walked to the paper section and picked up a copy of one of those lurid tabloids:

11

BABY BORN PREGNANT!
Top Doctors Baffled!

Kay began to flip through it.

"What are you *doing*?"

Kay put the tabloid back on the rack, removed another one.

Jay saw the headline on this one:

MAN EATS HIS OWN HOUSE!
And That's Just the Appetizer!!

"Man, I'd sure hate to be sued by the pope. That can't do you any good when you get to the Pearly Gates now, can it."

Kay kept flipping through the paper.

"Hello? Earth to Kay?"

Kay put that one back, reached for another one.

"Kay? You're not telling me *these* are the hotsheets?"

"Best damn investigative reporting there is," Kay said.

"You're pulling my chain again, aren't you?"

"You think so? You know what we do for a living. When was the last time you read about aliens in *The New York Times*?" He shook his head. "Those guys don't have a clue. Now *these* guys"—he waved the tabloid—"these guys are at least on the right track."

"You are actually looking for tips in supermarket *tabloids*. I cannot believe it."

"Not looking, Slick, *found*."

Kay held the paper up for Jay to see the story on the inside:

FARM WIFE SAYS "ALIEN STOLE MY HUSBAND'S SKIN!"
Spaceship Crushes Family Truck, Husband Vanishes!!

Jay looked up at the ceiling, said, "Help me, Spock."

"Come on," Kay said. "We're going to take a little ride in the country."

Edgar sat in the cockpit of the Zap-Em vehicle and sucked up dark fizzy liquid through a thin plastic tube—a straw, the tube was, another of those words whose definition made no sense. The liquid was called Jolt Cola, and while undeniably weak on the sugar content, it was better than nothing. He looked at himself in the small reflective device that allowed him to see to the rear of the vehicle, noticed a small flap of skin dangling from his neck. The skin tag was turning grayish and getting a bit crusty. He reached up and peeled it off. This costume wasn't going to last much longer without another spit-coat, inside and out, a prospect he did not relish. Sooner he could get done and get out of this fleshboy monkey suit, the better. But there was no denying it, if he didn't get it done fairly soon, he *would* have to fix the costume or it wouldn't hold together.

But maybe it wouldn't have to. For even as he thought this, he saw the door open—what was it named again? ah, the *jewelry store,* he recalled—and the one known as Rosenberg emerged.

Ah.

Rosenberg was an older model, and he carried two items. One appeared to be an intricately carved box. The other was a small, furry animal Edgar identified as a cat. It was sometimes the custom on this world for the higher mammals to keep lower orders—mammalian, reptilian, avian, or piscean—as pets. Sometimes these pets served a useful function, to rid the owner's domicile of yet smaller destructive mammalian or insectoid pests, but often these pets had no duties save to act as some kind of companion. There were two main species that fulfilled this role, cats and dogs, though some of the terran ruling class also kept more exotic creatures.

This symbiotic relationship seemed rather pointless to Edgar, but he supposed that if times got lean, the terrans probably utilized their pets as food, which did make a kind of sense. Saved them having to go out and hunt prey. As far as he was able to determine, humans were lousy hunters.

Rosenberg set the cat upon the box, then attended to the locking mechanisms on the door of the jewelry store. There appeared to be five such devices. When finished with his ministrations upon the door, he picked up the cat and box, and walked away.

Edgar started the vehicle and allowed it to idle along slowly, following the walker. He had to see where Rosenberg was going.

A yellow vehicle behind Edgar blasted its horn but Edgar ignored it and the stream of profanity the pilot-driver emitted in regard to Edgar's less than optimum pace. In due course, he would lean out, reply in kind, and offer the finger salute as was appropriate, but for now, he must take care not to lose sight of Rosenberg. Thus far, his mission had been relatively easy, and while he expected no less, it would not pay to become complacent. The path to victory was fraught with peril and a wise traveler kept himself alert to potential dangers.

Even though he could hardly conceive of any *real* problems on this dinky planet, it was better to be cautious than cauterized.

The Zap-Em vehicle rolled slowly along. The driver behind him cursed loudly, bespeaking itself mostly in regard to Edgar's ancestors and his unusual relationships with them, among other colorful descriptions.

All was in good order.

"Why don't you let me drive?" Jay asked Kay.

"I don't think you're quite ready for this car yet."

"Hey, I got a B in Driver's Ed."

"I'm sure you did. I got an A and I've been doing it longer."

"How much farther is it? Are we almost there yet? I need to go pee. I'm hungry. Can we stop at the souvenir shop?" Jay grinned.

Kay just shook his head.

"Almost there" was somewhere in upstate New York. The last hour or so had been in country so rural Jay couldn't believe it. Cows, horses, big empty fields, woods. It was pretty amazing. You sort of didn't think about New York having any real country.

He remarked upon this to Kay, who finally chuckled.

"You need to get out of the city more. But don't worry, you will."

The road wound through the trees, getting narrower and ruttier. By the time they actually got to their destination, they might as well have been in the middle of outer Mongolia or somewhere. There was one house, not much bigger than a double-wide trailer. And what appeared to be the smashed, scattered, burned-out remains of a pickup, upon which a large and heavy weight seemed to have fallen, sinking through the truck a few feet right into the gravel driveway.

Whatever had done the damage was not apparent.

"Looks like his truck overheated," Jay said.

Kay pulled the LTD to a stop.

Jay reached for the door handle.

"Hold up a second," he said. "Let's give the lady of the house time to wonder a little. Makes the job easier if they're a bit off balance."

After about a minute, a woman appeared in the doorway of the little house. Calling her "plain" would be a kindness. She wore lipstick, too bright, too red, and too much of it, and had rouged and powdered her face. "Can I help you gentlemen?" she called out.

"Now," Kay said.

They got out of the car and started up the driveway. As they walked, Kay pulled a card from his wallet. Jay glanced at the card, which looked like a blank, black credit card.

As Jay watched, the card in Kay's hand morphed into a leather badge holder with a very official-looking FBI ID card and badge in it.

"I *want* one of *those*," he told Kay.

"Maybe when you're older."

Kay waved the badge holder at the woman, then tucked it away. "How do you do, ma'am. I am Special Agent Manheim, this is Special Agent Black, we're with the FBI. We have a few questions we'd like to ask you."

"You here to make fun of me, too?"

"No, ma'am. We at the FBI don't have a sense of humor that we are aware of. May we come in?

The woman led them to the house, into a tiny kitchen. "Care for some lemonade?"

"Yes, ma'am, that would be nice," Kay said.

The woman got them glasses. To Jay it looked like dishwater with a yellow tinge. He smiled at her when he took the glass.

"So tell us about your husband, Mrs., ah . . . ?"

"Yax, Beatrice Yax. Come on into the living room."

They followed her. Kay took a sip of the drink she'd prepared and from his face, it must have tasted pretty bad. Jay resolved to let his drink evaporate.

He checked out the room while Beatrice Yax told her story. He listened with half his attention as he wandered over to the TV set and looked at the picture on top of it: a man, smiling, squatting and about to skin a presumably dead deer on the ground.

"That's my husband, that's Edgar, there in that picture."

Jay shook his head. Mr. Yax wasn't gonna win no prizes for beauty, either.

"—and so the Shurf said, 'Well, Miz Yax, if Edgar was dead' "—this word came out as a New Englander's 'dayudd'—" 'how was it he was able to walk back into the house?' "

"That does sound somewhat unusual," Kay offered.

"Well, yes, it does," Beatrice said. "I was stumped by that myself, but I know Edgar and even though it looked just like him, it wasn't *him*, if you know what I mean."

Kay raised his eyebrows.

"It was like he was wearing a suit," she said. "Only thing was, *he* was the suit. His skin, I mean. It was like an Edgar suit."

"I see. Make a note of that, Agent Black."

"I got it," Jay said.

"Did this person in the Edgar suit say anything, Miz Yax?"

"He said the truck got blowed up by sugar, but then he said what he wanted was some sugar. In water."

Kay nodded. "Sugar water. I see."

He took out his sunglasses, waved them at Jay. "Put your Ray·Bans on, there, would you, Slick?"

Jay shrugged. Pulled the issue glasses out and slipped them on.

Kay put his own glasses on and smiled at the woman.

"So, are you going to track this alien down and punish him for what he did to the truck? And Edgar?"

"Oh, yes, ma'am, you can rest assured of that." He pulled that little tape recorder thing Jay had seen him play with a couple of times. Pointed it at the woman. "Look here a second, would you, Miz Yax?"

The woman looked. There came a flash of light, bright even through the shades, and the woman's face went blank.

Kay took his glasses off, waved them at Jay to indicate he should do the same. Jay shrugged and complied.

Kay turned back to Mrs. Yax. "Now, Beatrice, listen carefully. There was no alien. That flash of light you saw wasn't a UFO hitting the truck, it was, oh, swamp gas that escaped from a weather balloon trapped in a thermal pocket that refracted the light from Venus. The truck had a leaky gas tank and that's what caused it to explode."

Jay frowned. "Whoa, hold up there. What'd you just do? What is that thing?"

"Standard issue neuralyzer," Kay said. "Erases memory in a subject, allows us to replace the blank spot with our own material."

"No shit? Cool. But—that's the best you can come up with? Swamp gas? Venus?"

Kay turned away from Jay and back to Mrs. Yax.

"Thing is, Beatrice, Edgar ran off with an old girlfriend. And after you go and stay with your mother for a few days, you'll not only get over it, you'll decide you're a lot better off without him."

"Yeah," Jay put in. "In fact, you *kicked* him out, and now that he's gone, you're gonna buy some new clothes, maybe redecorate the place and find somebody worthy of you."

He looked at Kay. "Might as well give the poor woman something."

Kay smiled at him. "I think you're getting the hang of it." He turned back to the woman. "One final thing, Beatrice. We were never here, so naturally, you wouldn't know us if you ever saw us again and you won't remember any of this conversation. And right now, you need to go take a little nap, for, oh say, a couple of hours, after which you'll feel a lot better."

Outside, Kay walked to the remains of the pickup truck and looked at it.

"How *did* the sucker get mashed like this?"

"Alien ship must have landed on it, just like it said in the paper. I'm telling you, those boys get the straight scoop more often than not."

"Uh-huh, I'm sure."

Kay continued. "Edgar came out to see what the fuss was about, the alien whacked him and took his body. Well. Probably disposed of most of it, just kept the skin."

"That happen a lot?"

"Nope. Mostly the legit visitors buy their disguises off-world, get them from MiB HQ, or at that little shop down in Greenwich Village—the one next to the place that makes those good fried egg sandwiches?"

"Hey, I know that place!"

"So, the fact that our visitor killed a local and swiped his skin for his mask, well, that's bad. That's pretty much a felony everywhere. Couple of worlds it's only a misdemeanor, but even so, it's not considered polite. So we're right away dealing with a criminal and not just somebody who hopped the fence."

He pulled another gadget from his pocket and pointed it at the crunched and fried truck. A thin beam flashed out and danced over the wreck and down into the depression.

"Now what?"

"Spectral analyzer. Picks up stray molecules a life form leaves behind. Kind of like an electronic bloodhound. See this little screen? It's color-coded to tell us what kind of alien we're dealing with."

"That's cute. What I want is one of them memory things. I know a couple of women I want to show it to."

"I bet." He waved the device. The little screen flashed, emitted a pulsing red light.

"We have a winner," Jay said. "It's a red-boy."

"Nope," Kay said. "It's not finished yet. Still sniffing."

Jay realized he was right, for as he watched, the spectral thing flashed again, yellow, this time.

Still, Kay kept waving it back and forth, and the next time it flashed, it was blue.

Kay was talking to the device he held: "Stop at purple," he said. "Don't go to green, okay?"

The device shifted to purple. Seemed to hold there.

"Thank you," Kay said.

But the toy pulsed for a couple of seconds . . . then the light changed to green.

Stayed green.

"Well, shit," Kay said. "Do you know what this means?"

Jay cut his gaze heavenward. "Wait, wait. Was this the last question on *Jeopardy!* last night? 'What kind of alien leaves a green spectral trail?' Hell no, I don't know what it means! I just got here."

Kay climbed out of the depression and headed for the car.

"You just gonna leave me hanging?" Jay said, following him. "What?"

At the car, Kay pulled what looked like an old-fashioned CB mike from under the dash and keyed it. Jay would bet diamonds to navel lint it wasn't any old-fashioned CB unit, though.

"Come on, man—?"

Kay waved him quiet.

"Zed? This is Kay."

"I'm here," came back from the radio.

"We're at the red letter landing site upstate."

"And you have good news for me . . . ?"

"Wishful thinking." He paused for a second, took a deep breath. Said, "We got a bug, Zed."

So there they were, upstate New York, looking at the remains of some yahoo's pickup truck and the damned reader had flashed green.

Big trouble.

The kid stood there as Kay racked the communicator's mike, and in that smart-ass way he had, said, "I'm gonna jump past you here and guess that a bug is a bad thing, is that right?"

Kay stared at him. Well, okay, he didn't know, he'd only been on the job just one day. Kay kept forgetting that. He and Dee would have already been on the road, cursing their luck, but he was going to have to explain things to the kid.

"Listen up, tiger. Bugs thrive on carnage. They consume, infest, infect, ruin, and destroy. They live off death and decay, and they are not above causing it so they can benefit."

12

"Is this a racial problem you have with all insect-based life forms?"

"Let me put it to you this way. Imagine, if you would, a T-rex-sized cockroach. This bug is smarter than you are, four times stronger than a full-grown ox, nine times meaner than hell, *and* it hates us. It hates our air, it hates our food, and it hates our architecture, all of which make it cranky. Now picture it walking around Manhattan in its brand new Edgar suit. Does this sound like a fun dance partner?"

"How did a giant cockroach get into a five-foot-something Edgar suit?"

"They got ways. And using those ways makes them even more cranky. A cranky bug is a death machine just waiting for somebody stupid enough to switch it on."

"So, all right, we got a bad dude. What do we do? How do we find it?"

"Get in the car. We have to get back to the city."

"What makes you think he—it—the bug-in-Edgar, whatever—is going to the city?"

Kay waved. "You see anything out here worth sticking around for? He'll go to the city. He's here to assassinate somebody. That's what bugs do."

"It's a big town. How are we going to find him?"

"We watch the morgues."

Rosenberg got out of a cab in front of an establishment entitled Leshko's. He carried with him still the cat and ornate box. He tendered the pilot of the cab some local currency—Edgar realized he probably needed to get some of that somewhere were he to be here much longer—and went into the building.

Edgar parked the truck and got out. He set the ship's alarm system to "disintegrate" and walked toward the building.

A quick scan revealed that Leshko's was an eatery: there were dozens of terrans seated at tables consuming colorful but foul-smelling foodstuffs. He saw Rosenberg approach a table at which was seated a large middle-aged man. Rosenberg set the box upon the table. The cat immediately leaped upon the box. The large man stood, he and Rosenberg exchanged formal embraces.

Aha. Not a terran, but someone wearing the disguise of one, as was Rosenberg. Exactly as he expected. Here were the ambassadors, easy as could be. Save for the ship, this had thus far been a perfect assignment.

He would dine out on this assignment for a long time.

Rosenberg seated himself across from the ersatz man.

Edgar thought fast. He needed to get into the eatery—restaurant, café, diner—without attracting attention, to positively confirm his suspicions. He observed the food servers. They were free to stand or move about without anyone paying them undue notice. Yes.

It was but the work of a few moments to amble around the back of the restaurant, find a waiter standing in the alley inhaling fragrant smoke from a thin white tube—a cigarette—kill him, and remove his clothing. Thus he wore a disguise over his disguise.

Edgar hurried in through the food preparation area and into the main dining area.

He arrived in the vicinity of Rosenberg's table. Now, how to confirm these two without arousing their suspicions?

An old human seated at the next table said, "Waiter!

It's about damned time! Are you ready to take my order?"

Edgar looked around, saw another server with a pad and writing device listening to a patron. Ah. He fished the new disguise's pocket and found a similar pad and writing device, removed them, and pretended to listen to the customer. This would give him an excuse to stand here.

"I'll have the pierogi. And do it right, you understand? Last time I was here, it was terrible."

Edgar nodded, but his attention was on the conversation at the next table. With his enhanced hearing, he was able to catch every word.

The two "men" spoke Arquillian.

"To peace," Rosenberg said.

"To peace," the disguised Arquillian said. For that was certainly who he was.

They raised their glasses of liquid, sipped at them.

The Arquillian said, "To think that after all this time, we should come together in a shithole like this."

Rosenberg smiled. "Earth? It's not so bad, once you get used to the smell."

The Arquillian set his glass upon the table. "All right, where is it?"

"Hello? Are you awake here, bub?" the customer seated in front of Edgar said. "Hello?"

Edgar focused part of his attention upon the customer. He replayed the conversation. "You said pierogi. Done right."

"Yes, I did. I also said beet soup and do that right, too."

"Beet soup."

"Last time I ate in here, the borscht was terrible."

"Terrible," Edgar echoed.

"You waited this long," Rosenberg said, still in fluent Arquillian. "Why don't we eat first?"

No, Edgar thought. *Don't eat first!* While he had enough to know that these were in fact the Baltian and Arquillian ambassadors, he needed one more thing—

There came a commotion from the food preparation area. From the tone of it, Edgar deduced that the body of the former owner of his waiter disguise had been found. He had stuffed it into a refuse bin, but it had not been a very good fit, even after he folded it in half. Next time, he should take better care. Humans seemed to get very disturbed at such occurrences, and doubtless they would be calling in the local authorities. While a few lightly armed terrans were no real threat to him, it was time to finish this business and move on. He had confirmed what he absolutely had to know.

"Are you deaf?" the customer said. "I said I wanted tea!"

Next to him, the Arquillian said, "All right. We'll eat. Then we'll drink again, to the return of the Third Galaxy to Arquillian rule."

To the customer, Edgar said, "Cease your brainless prattling or I will kill you."

The customer's eyes went wide.

One of the little fathers, a long silvery multilegged being with pinchers at its tail, fell from Edgar's sleeve upon the table. After a moment, several other of the small ones he had rescued from the Zap-Em's attempts to slay them also decided to leave Edgar's disguise. They, too, fell upon the table. Their choice, of course. He would not compel them to stay.

The customer departed in a great hurry.

Next to him, the Arquillian and Rosenberg looked at

Edgar. He saw them look at the insects and arachnids, then realize that he was not what he appeared to be. Oh, well. No more time for subtle gestures. He dropped the pad and writing instrument and turned toward the two.

Rosenberg said, "You can kill us both, but it won't stop the peace."

Edgar forced the disguise's face into a smile. "Well. You are correct about one thing."

He extruded his stinger, fired it under the table, hit Rosenberg and then the Arquillian each with a jolt of venom. Both of them lurched forward and fell facedown upon the table. He retracted the stinger.

He began rummaging through the dead creatures' clothing. Where is it, where *is* it—?

The noise in the food serving area increased. A terry emerged through the swinging door, pointed at Edgar, and yelled, "There he is!"

More terrans came through the door. Two of them were armed with cutting implements.

Nothing in the dead ambassadors' clothing pouches. Blast! Where *was* it—?

Ah. The box!

Edgar reached for the box. The cat upon it hissed at him and bared its teeth. He did not have time for this. Edgar batted the cat aside. It flew a short distance and landed on the meal set before a female terry, much to her surprise and dismay.

Doubtless the cat had not enjoyed its short flight, either. Too bad for both of them.

The humans with the cutting implements approached. Some of the other patrons rose to their feet and began yelling. Greatly hampered in his movements as he was by the fleshy disguise, Edgar knew it was better to leave than indulge himself in the slaughter of them all. He had killed the two ambassadors and the box surely contained that which he wanted.

Much as he would have liked to stay and play, the mission was paramount.

Edgar clutched the box tightly and ran for the exit. The two terrans stupid enough to stand in his way regretted it. He shouldered them aside with enough force to knock them sprawling.

Behind him, the cat howled and hissed.

As he ran toward the Zap-Em vehicle, Edgar felt a great personal satisfaction. Were this assignment any easier, why, he could have commed it in from his nest.

He disarmed the ship's alarm, opened the door of the Zap-Em vehicle, and tossed the box inside. He climbed into the cockpit and used the key to start the engine. He pulled out into the line of traffic, made the universal hand gesture at a pilot who horned at him, and drove away.

Dr. Laurel Weaver was busy cataloging the numerous knife wounds on the corpse of the knife-fight victim when a uniformed cop came in, accompanying her orderly, who was pushing a gurney.

She glanced up, then back at her current client.

The body on her table, who had been a body-builder when he was still breathing, to judge from the size of his muscles, had "Blood Vipers" and "Hoover Kick Dogs" tattooed on his chest. He also had several other meaningless-to-her symbols tattooed on his chest, back, buttocks, and ankles. The names of at least eight women adorned one arm, and seven of them had tattooed lines drawn through them. Into monogamy, this guy?

Somebody had stuck a thin knife blade neatly though all the letter O's in the chest tattoos.

115

Cute.

"And here is yet another customer," the cop said. "Just a little off the top and sides, okay? I think he's in a hurry."

Laurel cut her gaze at him. Cops thought they were so funny, every one of them.

"Busy night," the cop said, grinning.

"Tell me about it." Laurel turned around. "Another drive-by?"

"Nah, this one got it in a Russian restaurant, got two more out in the hall from the same location."

"Great. Now all I need is a train wreck or an Italian wedding."

She waved at the new arrival. "Put him against the wall—hello? What's with the cat?"

The cat sat on the foot of the gurney, glaring as only a cat can at the orderly and cop.

"Apparently belonged to the victim," the cop said. "It was in the restaurant. I need you to sign here."

He passed a clipboard to Laurel.

"Remind me not to eat wherever this guy died." She jotted her name down on the form. "So, what are you going to do with the cat?"

"I'm not going to do anything with it. It's your problem now."

"Hey—"

"You signed for it. Feed it some liver or kidneys or something. You probably got some lying around you ain't using. See ya, lady."

The cop and the orderly left. After a moment, the orderly came back wheeling two gurneys, pushing one and pulling the other.

"Showing off again, Tom?"

"Yes, ma'am."

Laurel walked over to the new stiffs and looked at them. The cat arched its back and rubbed up against her hip. She petted it. "You having a bad day, baby?" Laurel said. "Me, too. But cheer up, *his* day is a lot worse."

She waved at the corpse.

She picked up the cat, set it on a surgical tray, and moved the gurney under the light. "Okay, let's just take a quick peek at your late owner, shall we?"

The corpse had a bluish tinge to it, froth at the corners of its mouth, bulging eyes, and swollen fingers. "Poison? What *was* the name of that restaurant, kitty?"

She pulled the sheet back, frowned at the nude body.

There was a large swelling on the left leg, near the groin. The flesh was an angry purple, surrounding what appeared to be at first glance a big-bore hypodermic injection site. It looked like nothing so much as a giant wasp sting. Or maybe a snakebite from a reptile with only one fang. Hmm. Interesting.

The second corpse, a bigger and younger man, also had that mark on him, a little higher. My, my.

The first body could wait, there was no doubt about what killed him. These were much more intriguing.

"Get this one on the table, would you, Tom?" She nodded at the bigger man.

"I thought you weren't supposed to break in line," the orderly said.

"I didn't hear anybody ahead of him complaining."

The orderly laughed. He shifted the body from the gurney onto the blood table, then left.

Laurel changed into a clean gown, double-gloved and remasked, turned the recorder on.

"The subject is a well-developed, well-nourished white male"—she looked at the paperwork the cop had left—"who appears to be about the stated age of fifty-two." She went on to measure and describe the subject's height, hair, eyes, and general characteristics, including the swollen puncture wound on his leg.

After that, it didn't take long for her to discover that what she had on the table wasn't what it appeared to be.

Not like any human being she had ever seen.

Laurel continued her work, more and more astounded. She tried to keep her voice calm and even for the recorder, but it was difficult.

"—oral temperature approximately one hundred and twelve degrees F. at the time of autopsy. Examiner attempted to verify this reading rectally only to find that the subject was, uh, that is, um . . . without a rectum. No anal opening apparent. Which can only be described as . . . um . . ."

"Weird?" came a voice from behind her. Laurel started. She turned and saw two men in ugly black suits standing in the doorway. One white, fifty-something, the other one young and black.

"Excuse me, what are you doing here?"

The older man stepped forward and held up an ID card.

"I'm Dr. Leo Menville, Department of Public Health. This is my associate, Dr. White."

Laurel looked at the ID. It had the man's name and picture on it, and the notation Special Investigator under it. Looked official enough, and if they'd gotten back here past Larry and Tom, they must be legit.

She nodded. Glanced up at the clock on the wall over the table. Lord, it was three in the morning.

She said, "You boys must not have much of a home life. How'd you find out about these two so fast?"

"It's our job," Menville said. "Why don't you fill us in, doctor?"

Laurel shook her head. "I wish I could. The three were apparently killed in a Russian restaurant. One of them, the waiter, looks normal enough, save for a broken spine. The other two, well, I don't know what to tell you. Take a look at this."

Menville moved over to look at the first body, the bigger man.

"I never saw a skeletal structure like this before."

"What killed him?"

"I have to wait for the tox screen, but offhand, I'd say he was poisoned. Injection, right there." She pointed at the wound.

"Same for the other one?"

"So it appears. I was just ready to start on him, only just got the incision done."

"Why don't you go ahead and work on him? Dr. White will assist you, if you don't mind. I'll poke around in this one a little."

Laurel nodded. It was late, she was tired, but this was pretty amazing. She welcomed the help, because she sure as hell didn't know what to make of these two.

She'd gone into this line of work because she didn't like the idea of her patients dying on her. There wasn't much you could do to hurt a guy who was already dead. And while she'd seen some pretty amazing things since she'd been on the job, nothing compared with this. Nothing.

"Gowns and gloves over there," she said to the young black doctor. He was kind of cute. Nice eyes. Seemed . . . familiar, somehow.

When "Dr. White" came back, gowned and gloved, Laurel led him to the corpse of the older man. She said,

119

"I just started the lap, but already I have a whole bunch of anomalies. Here, check this out."

White looked a little reticent to begin digging into the lap. She smiled, mostly to herself. Probably he hadn't played with a cadaver since medical school, if he was in epidemiology. A number cruncher, all into statistics. She understood that. People thought if you were a doctor, you knew everything there was to know about medicine and that wasn't real bright. That, after all, was why there were so many specialists: would you want a dermatologist doing neurosurgery on you? She couldn't remember the number of times people had come up to her at a party and started asking for free medical advice. When she told them she was a coroner, that usually shut them up, but not always. An M.D. is an M.D., right?

Yeah. Sure.

"Jump right in, doctor, I'm pretty sure he won't mind."

The young black doctor put his hand into the body cavity.

"What am I looking for?"

Definitely squeamish, this guy. But cute.

"Notice anything strange about the stomach, liver, the lungs?"

"Nope. All fine."

Geez, how long had it been since he was in medical school? He was young, couldn't be any longer than it had been for her. "They are all *missing*, doctor."

"I *know* that. What I mean is that there aren't any pieces of them left, so they are all *intact* wherever they are."

She said, "Have we met before? Your eyes seem familiar."

"Funny, I was about to ask you the same thing."

He was familiar, but there was no memory of him. She wouldn't have forgotten, she was sure of that.

She leaned over. "You want to know what I think? Not to geek out your senior physician or anything, he looks pretty stressed, but I don't think this is a body at all."

"Really?"

"No, I think it's some kind of . . . I don't know, some kind of . . . transport system. Kind of like a . . . an organic *car* or something. Question is—what is it supposed to transport? And where is it, whatever *it* is?"

He swallowed.

"Been a while since you did one of these, hey?"

"Uh, yeah. A while. We don't get a lot of bodies at the office, you know."

The older doctor cleared his throat. "Jay? A moment?"

The young guy jerked his gloved hands out of the corpse so fast it looked like they were on springs. "Be right there."

Laurel grinned and continued her exploration of the whatever-it-was. This was going to be worth a paper for *JAMA* or the *New England Journal of Medicine,* easy.

"What do you think?" Kay asked.

Jay didn't have to go far to answer that one. "Very interesting. Queen of the undead kind of thing."

"I meant the body."

"Great body, far as I can tell—"

"The *dead* body," Kay said. He sighed.

"Oh, that. Haven't got a clue."

"Truer words probably never spoken. All right. Keep her occupied for a couple more minutes. Try not to sound too dumb."

"Moi? Surely you jest?"

"No, I don't. And don't call me Shirley."

"Oh, man. Boo. Boo."

"Dr. White?"

"Man," Jay said, "I can't believe you said that. That joke's so old it's got Noah's footprints all over it."

"Dr. White?"

"Wait long enough," Kay said, "and wide ties'll come back in style."

"Sheeit—"

"Dr. White!"

Jay turned and looked at the woman.

"That's you. You're up, slugger."

"Oh, yeah. Forgot." He hurried across the room toward Laurel.

"Sorry," he said. "My boss was pulling my chain."

"Take a look at this."

Jay looked. There was something around the base of the stiff's ear, looked like stitching or something. He reached out, touched the ear. Had a sudden inspiration. He twisted the ear like a car radio knob.

The ear came away from the head as if it were a latch.

"Shit!" Laurel said.

"I hear that," Jay said.

He tugged on the ear again. All of a sudden, the dead Rosenberg's whole face kind of . . . pushed out. There was a mechanical hum as it slid forward then hinged open, the face rotating away like a mask from the skull.

And in the center of the hollow skull was—was—

A little green man sitting there!

122

Jay said a word that he normally didn't use in mixed company.

The green dude sat in a padded chair inside a tiny control room, complete with viewscreens and what looked like itty-bitty computers and all. The little green man was in bad shape, that was apparent. He gasped, wheezed, motioned for Jay and Laurel to lean closer.

They did.

The green man said, "Must—must to—prevent . . ." He trailed off, seemed to be searching for a word. "Contest? No, no, word for—deadly competition?"

"Struggle?" Jay said.

"War?" Laurel said.

The little green man nodded. "Y-Y-Yes. Prevent war! You—you must—galaxy . . ."

He ran out of air.

"What about the galaxy?" Jay asked.

"Galaxy. On . . . Orion's beh-beh-beh—?"

"Orion's what? Bed? Baby? Belt?"

"Yes! B-B-Belt, ah!"

The tiny green man slumped over.

Jay looked at Laurel.

"I think he's dead," Laurel said.

"To prevent war, the galaxy on Orion's belt? What does that mean?" Jay said.

"Who the hell cares?" she said. "Look at this! It's an *alien*! Here, right here, in my exam room! A little green man!"

"A *dead* little green man," Jay said. "Kay! I mean, uh, Doctor, uh, uh, whatever! Get over here!"

Laurel leaned back and stared at Jay. "Dr. Whatever? You don't remember your boss's name? You're not with

Public Health. Who the hell are you? What the hell is going on here?" She waved at the little green guy.

Kay came over, looked at the stiff. Make that stiffs, plural, Jay thought. Or a stiff in a car with a dead battery or something. Too weird, all this. Really.

"Rosenberg," Kay said. "Too bad. One of the few I really liked. A supposedly exiled Baltian High Prince, but I bet that was just his cover. Doing some freelance ambassador work here, I bet."

Laurel said, "An alien life form and you're from some secret government agency!"

They ignored her. Jay said, "He said something like, 'to prevent war, the galaxy is on Orion's belt.' "

Laurel said, "Aliens. Here on Earth. Ah. This would explain so much about New York! The cabs!"

Kay pointed, said to Jay, "Look at that."

Jay looked down. Felt rather than saw the flash behind his back.

Kay said, "There's a galaxy on Orion's belt? That doesn't make any sense. Orion is in our galaxy."

"That's what the man—the Baltian, whatever—said. Ask her." He turned.

Laurel had a glazed look on her face. Oops. "What did you do?" Jay asked.

Laurel said, "Uh, hi, whoever you are. I'm going to need to see some ID if you're going to be here, okay?"

"Sure, sweetheart, here you go. Jay, look over there."

Jay looked.

Flash.

"Damn, Kay—"

Kay, shades in place—when had he done that?—said to Laurel, "It's been a typical day, too much caffeine, not enough rest. Nothing unusual about any of the stiffs today, including the three from the Russian restaurant, all dead of gunshots, send 'em to Potter's Field, usual chain-of-evidence all logged in. Forget us and everything we've said or are about to say. Lose the next five minutes altogether."

Jay said, "That thing makes me nervous. Probably gives you brain cancer or something."

"Didn't hurt her before."

"Before? How many times you done the flashy thing to this poor woman?"

"Couple. A few."

"You aren't worried about long-term mental damage?"

"Well. A little bit. But what can you do?"

"You a callous son-of-a-bitch. How'd you get like this?"

"I got recruited into this job. Come on, time to leave."

Laurel stood there, still dazed.

"What about her?"

"She'll be all right. Come on."

Jay had a sudden suspicion. "You never flashed *me* with that sucker, did you?"

"Now why would you think that? You're one of us now."

Jay shook his head.

Outside the morgue, Kay led Jay toward their car.

"How about you let me take care of the flashy memory thing for a while?"

"I don't think so, Slim."

"You don't trust me?"

"In a word, no."

"That hurts, Kay, it really does. I'm one of us now, remember?"

"Uh-huh. Well, I'm more us than you are. Maybe when you're older." Kay grinned. He really did like this kid. He was gonna work out fine, once he got a little experience under his belt.

The MiB containment vehicle pulled up and four agents got out.

Kay said, "We've got two dead extees inside who need to go bye-bye and a deputy medical coroner who might need a little touch-up. Be gentle with the woman. Jay here has a thing for her."

Jay glared at him.

The four MiB agents grinned as one.

"Come on, Jay. We got places to go and aliens to catch."

"You cold, Kay. A cold man."

"Like a tub full of liquid nitrogen at the South Pole, hoss," Kay said. "You want warm and cuddly, go back chasing pimps and crackheads for the po-lice. You can't get involved in people's lives in this job. It just gets in the way."

Night, but dwindling rapidly toward morning in the place called New York City. Soon the primary star would rise and the day cycle would begin again.

There were fewer humans on the sidewalks and streets, but the streets and walks could hardly be called deserted. The lights on poles, buildings, from signs and such banished the darkness and made the place brighter than a lot of worlds he'd been on in what passed for their days.

Humans were afraid of the dark, so he guessed that explained it.

Not that he was feeling the need to ponder such philosophical inquiries. No. Seated inside the Zap-Em vehicle, Edgar was more than a little upset. The box he'd taken from the dead Baltian was more than the simple plant fiber-construct it appeared to be. The bedamned Baltian had concealed under the wood a cube of duraconium and the dense and hard metal had resisted all of Edgar's attempts to open it.

He growled and hammered the box with the disguise's fist. The wood covering split again and again but the duraconium was undamaged. Blast! Curse all Baltians to the Eternal Desert!

He couldn't continue to treat the disguise this way— it was fragile enough that it would tear and then he'd have to get a new one, a prospect he found distasteful in the extreme.

He rummaged around and found a metal implement in the small storage compartment in the vehicle's dashboard, said implement being a yellow plastic handle from which a single metal bar, flattened on the end, extended. A screwdriver. He used this device to try to pry the box open.

He smacked the plastic handle of the screwdriver— what was a screw? Why did you have to drive it anywhere? How did you do that with this instrument?— hard with his fleshy hand. The metal bar *grinched* but did little to pry open the box.

Edgar cursed in his native tongue, consigning the box, the Baltians, life, the universe, and everything to eternal damnation in the lowest of the Seventeen Dry Pits *beneath* the Eternal Desert. He slammed the box repeatedly against the door of the Zap-Em vehicle, screaming in wordless anger.

The few passersby on the sidewalk glanced fearfully at the Zap-Em vehicle but none dared approach closely. Just as well they did not. Feeling as he did, Edgar would have slaughtered legions, had they come within reach. At least that many. Maybe more. Stupid gerking humans!

A final smash against the door brought a partial result. One corner of the inner box gaped a hair.

Aha!

He retrieved the drivescrewer and jammed the tip into the gap. With great effort, even for him, he managed to lever the gap wider, until at last the locking device gave up the battle.

The lid sprang open.

"Ha! I have you now!" Edgar said.

Inside, the box was filled with faceted, glittering stones. Green ones, red ones, clear ones. Decorative gems, he realized, humans being so fond of such glittery objects they had entire shops dedicated to the buying and selling of them. Baubles mostly offered to females to effect mating rituals, as nearly as he could tell.

Nothing else inside.

Edgar's rage flared white hot and he screamed so loudly that the window of the door upon which he had bashed the box shattered from the pitch of his angered voice:

"Nooooooo!"

Damn, damn, damn, *damn!*

It wasn't *here!*

This was bad. Very bad. It had all gone so well he should have known something would happen. It always did, he *never* had things easy.

Why was his life so much harder than everyone else's? It wasn't fair!

When Jay and Kay got back to headquarters, it was like 5:00 A.M. As far as Jay could tell, everybody who'd been there yesterday when he had left was still there—the place was running at full blast.

The big-screen TV, or whatever it was, now displayed a constellation of stars, even one Jay could recognize: Orion.

He said as much to Kay.

"City boy like you recognizes that?"

"Summer camp in Pennsylvania."

Zed cruised over and looked at them.

Jay said, "Nobody believes in sleep around here?"

"The twins keep us on Centaurian time." He nodded at the twin aliens. "Thirty-seven-hour day. You get used to it, save for the occasional psychotic episode."

"That explains a lot," Jay said.

Zed pulled a laser pointer and put the little red dot onto the screen. "Orion, pretty much the brightest grouping of stars in the northern skies. And here"—he waggled the pointer—"here is Orion's belt."

"So this is what the little green guy was talking about. The galaxy on Orion's belt?"

Zed shook his head. "There *aren't* any galaxies on Orion's belt. There are just these three stars and they aren't lined up neatly like they appear, they only look that way from Earth. Galaxies are made up of *billions* of stars." He switched off the pointer. "You heard it wrong."

Jay smiled. "You're attracted to me, aren't you? I understand. I won't hold it against you."

Zed frowned at him.

"I might be the new kid on the block and don't know squat but there ain't nothing wrong with my ears. That's what he said, that's what I heard. I had a witness but the iceman zapped her brain."

Jay looked to see if Kay had gotten the dig, but the older man wasn't around—ah, there he was. Over by a smaller monitor. Damn, he'd even loosened his tie.

"Check you later," Jay said.

He drifted over to where Kay sat. Peered over his shoulder.

On the monitor was a map of North America that shifted as it zoomed in on Arizona, then a city, then a block, and then right into somebody's backyard.

"Nice lens," Jay said.

Kay ignored him. The screen flashed: "Subject Acquired," it said.

The zoom focused on a middle-aged woman. The screen flashed more words:

SUBJECT: ELIZABETH ANN RESTON. PRESENT LOCATION: RESIDENCE.

ADDRESS: 553 FAIRFIELD AVENUE / TEMPE / ARIZONA / USA.

Jay looked at the woman. "Nice-looking," he said. "For a woman her age."

Kay's expression was hard to read, but there was something in it. Like . . . longing?

Jay made an intuitive connection. There was no other reason but that, intuition, but he was sure he was right. "Damn," he said.

Kay looked at him.

"That's her, ain't it? The girl who never got the flowers from that young guy in the pictures I saw. You. And you still keep track after all these years?"

Kay said nothing.

"You must have really had a thing for her. She ever get married?"

"No," Kay said. The pain in his voice was the most emotion he'd shown since they'd met.

So. Dude wasn't as cold as he let on. Maybe all that stuff with the Doc got to him. Maybe he was just putting on a tough front. Hell, everybody knew that Spock had human feelings, no matter how much he tried to deny it. Damn.

Kay reached out, touched a control. The screen scrambled.

SUBJECT LOST

Kay leaned back in the chair.

Lord, Jay thought. *Is this gonna be me in thirty years?*

Jay said, "Well, it's better to have loved and lost—"

Kay turned and impaled him with a glare. Jay shut up. Well. Maybe this was not the time to bring that up. If looks could kill, he'd be a smoking spot on the floor. Later. They could talk about all this later, when they got to know each other better. Maybe in ten or fifteen years.

Zed said, "Kay? Over here."

Zed had that resident alien display lit up on the screen again. Jay and Kay moved over to look at it. The lists were flickering. Some of them went out.

"They're leaving," Kay said. His voice was filled with a kind of amazed dread.

"Twelve jumps in the last hour alone," Zed said. "Redgick and his wife and new kid were just ahead of the curve."

"How come they're leaving?" Jay asked. "What do they know that we don't?"

Kay looked at him, then back at the screen. "How do rats know to desert a sinking ship?" To the twins, he said, "Go to Lem Sat Four. Put up a forty-field view of Manhattan, please."

On the screen, a bright spot of light on the East Coast that represented New York City blinked on. Kay said, "Go to four hundred."

The picture changed into a view of the Earth from space.

"Four thousand," Kay said. "Give me a scan."

Now the image shifted to a longer view of the planet, it was just a marble-sized blue ball hanging there. A tiny dot flashed off to one side. Under it, the words "Level Four." The image shifted, centered on the blinking dot.

"Oh, shit," Kay said. "When did that get here?"

Zed shook his head. "Wasn't there on the morning scan."

"What?" Jay said. "What?"

"That's an Arquillian battle cruiser," Kay said.

"And we've got ourselves a dead Arquillian prince," Zed said.

A sound like a cat and a mouse caught in a blender came from the speakers mounted next to the screen.

"Incoming communication from the battle cruiser," one of the twins said. That's what Jay thought she said.

"Run it through the translator," Zed said. He looked at Kay. "We've been having some problems with the translator."

"They sound pissed," Jay observed.

"They are," Kay said. "If they weren't, they wouldn't be here."

Zed turned to Kay. "Better get down to Rosenberg's store and see what you can turn up. Go well armed. Whatever the bug is up to is bad and I *really* don't like seeing this cruiser hanging out there."

"Nobody is gonna say anything about having a bad feeling about this, are they?" Jay said.

"Shut up," Zed said. "Go."

Kay nodded. He led Jay down the hall to the equipment locker. From out of a lock box he opened with his hand print, he pulled a multibarreled handgun, a weird sucker with a little clear canister under it that looked like a fuel-line trap on an old pickup truck. Some kind of gas swirled in the canister, different colors. Nasty-looking piece of hardware.

"Nice toy," Jay said. "What is it?"

"A Series Four deatomizer." He pulled a holster out, slipped it onto his belt, and stuck the big gun into it. Then he rummaged around in the locker again and came out with another gun. This one was so tiny you could hide it in your hand.

"Here," Kay said. "We call this the Noisy Cricket."

Jay took the gun. Looked like a kid's toy. A real small kid. "*You* get the Series Four deatomizer and *I* get a Noisy Cricket? C'mon!"

Kay ignored him.

On the way out, they passed by the big screen again. Now there was a close-up shot of the whatchamacallit battle cruiser. Thing had a lot of tubes sticking out of it. As he watched, the tubes moved, lined up all pointed in the same direction.

"Those guns?" Jay asked.

"Yep."

"They just pointed them at something."

"Yep."

"Do I want to know what?"

"Not really."

Outside on the way to the car, Jay thought it might be a good idea to lighten things up a little. "You know, when you said we couldn't form any attachments, you didn't mean *no attachments at all*, did you? I mean, if you see where I'm going here, if I'm not ever going to be able to kick back and have, you know, a *friend* over to visit, I might have to renegotiate my contract here."

Kay cracked a thin smile.

He glanced up at the sky, dawn beginning to color it with light. "That cruiser up there got a lot of fire-power?"

"Enough to turn Earth into a burned-out cinder in less time than it takes to blink."

"Oh, Lord. They wouldn't shoot us, would they?"

"Maybe not. Then again, the Arquillians really take exception to having their people murdered. And they don't have a particularly high opinion of humans. If we don't catch the bug who killed their guy PDQ, I wouldn't start any long books, if I were you."

"Damn," Jay said.

"Amen."

Edgar arrived in the vicinity of the bauble shop from which he had followed Rosenberg. There were no empty slots next to the sidewalk wherein he could park the Zap-Em vehicle, so he pulled up next to an automobile occupying one of the slots and stopped his vehicle's motor. Should the pilot of the automobile wish to depart before Edgar finished his business, well, too bad. He would just have to wait.

There seemed to be plenty of precedent—other vehicles were so parked and no one seemed to be bothering them.

Edgar walked to the shop. He smashed the glass of the window, reached inside and undid the locking mechanisms, of which there were several, opened the door, and entered.

A loud and blaring ringing filled the air. He ignored it, began to search.

15

Everywhere were gems, ornate and portable time-pieces, glittery bands of precious metals. How savage these creatures were, to feel the need to bedeck themselves with such ornate trash.

He broke display cases, tossed the gems aside, searching.

Nothing! Nothing!

His anger unleashed, Edgar smashed everything he could reach. He ripped pictures from the wall, flat, nonholo images of various subjects, and shattered them against whatever came to hand.

At the third or fourth of these portraits, he stopped. The one he held was of the small creature the Rosenberg had carried. Edgar looked around. Several of the images were of the creature—the cat.

Hmm. Obviously this animal was of some importance to the disguised off-worlder. . . .

There came a new beeping sound from outside, loud enough to penetrate Edgar's consciousness even over the blaring alarm inside the store. He looked out through the shattered glass.

A large vehicle had come to a stop in front of the Zap-Em truck. The pilot had alighted and was connecting what appeared to be some kind of towing cable device to the Zap-Em truck. Edgar frowned. Best he take care of this.

Outside, Edgar approached the human.

"What do you think you're doing?"

"You can't double-park here, pal. Pick it up at the impound at Twenty-third and Pier."

"You cannot take this vehicle. I have need of it."

"Life is hard."

Edgar looked around. There were a number of humans about, although most of them paid no mind to the shattered glass, the strident alarm, or the pilot and Edgar. Probably not a good idea to rip the human's limbs off and draw unwanted attention. He needed to be more subtle.

Edgar went to his vehicle, removed from it the weapon the Edgar had attempted to use on him immediately after his landing.

He returned to where the human continued to connect the two vehicles. He waved the shotgun at the pilot. "Look at this," Edgar said.

"Nice. What's that, a twelve-gauge? I got worse in the truck, pal." He continued to connect the towing device, ignoring the threat of imminent death.

Were these humans stupid, or what? Could not the feeble-brained creature see he was in danger? Did he not care?

In the LTD, Jay had been careful to buckle his seat belt before Kay started the engine. He felt a little better as they drove the streets of Manhattan, inching through gridlock after gridlock. This was a terrible town to waste a car on, even a relic like this Fix-Or-Repair-Daily Detroit dinosaur iron.

"You know, I must admit I kinda liked that medical examiner."

Kay glanced over at him. "I kinda noticed."

"Thing is, once you zapped her, she forgot all about me."

"Lucky for you. I never saw a black man turn green, not until you got to fiddling with that alien harbinger."

"Alien whosits?"

"Harbinger. The disguises some aliens wear are flesh,

alive, after a fashion, but they aren't really human, as young Dr. Laurie noticed in a hurry. There is a sort of symbiotic relationship between the body and the entity controlling it, kind of like a horse and rider. The rider feeds the horse and combs it, gives it a place to sleep, and the horse carries him where he wants to go. It's kind of like that. Sort of."

"Yeah, well, the innards felt slimy enough to be real."

"My point. You didn't impress Dr. Laurie with your cast-iron stomach, now did you? Better she should forget you were on the edge of spewing your dinner all over her nice clean autopsy room. That way, if you ever see her again, you can start out fresh."

"She won't remember me at all?"

"Probably not. Sometimes the neuralyzer leaves a little bit of synapse, so there's a kind of familiarity, a little déjà vu, but mostly it wipes memories clean. And there are stories that there are a few people who are immune, or partially immune, but I can't say I've run into any of them. Whoops, here we are. Rosenberg's Jewelry, dead ahead."

Jay said, "Guess that describes ole Rosenberg and that little green man, all right."

Jay saw a man in the street next to a double-parked Zap-Em truck arguing with a tow truck operator, looked like some hayseed come to the city. He grinned. Guy sure didn't know shit if he thought he was gonna talk his way out of getting his truck hauled off. New York tow truck operators were more used to dangerous shit than 7-Eleven clerks working the stickup shift, and that was saying something.

"Uh-oh," Kay said.

"You know I don't like hearing you say that. What?"

"Take a look."

Jay looked at the jewelry store. The front window was smashed, the door wide open.

"Okay, *I'll* say it. I got a bad feeling about this, Obi-wan," Jay said.

Kay pulled the LTD into a slot vacated by a deli wagon and got out. He stuck his hand under his coat. Had it, no doubt, on that big-ass pistol. Jay put his own hand into his jacket pocket and found the tiny little gun he carried. It didn't offer him much comfort. What kind of name was Noisy Cricket? You pulled the trigger and it chirped? Gee-zus.

Kay went in first, pulled his gun as soon as he was off the street. Jay was right behind him.

The place was trashed, diamonds and rubies and shit spilled all over like a ripped-open sack of dog food. Must have been a couple hundred thousand bucks in merchandise just lying on the floor.

"What kind of fool robs a jewelry store and leaves the jewels behind?" Jay said.

Kay put his gun away. Jay looked at the cricket gun, shook his head, put it back into his pocket.

Kay said, "Somebody who's not looking for jewels."

Jay looked at the pictures on the floor and still on the wall. "Man had a serious crush on his cat, didn't he?"

"Not a man," Kay said. "An alien. Try not to forget that."

Jay looked around. Caught movement from outside the store. That hayseed arguing with the tow truck guy was moving in their direction and two things hit Jay at once: He knew that face from somewhere. And—the guy had a shotgun in his hands.

"Down!" Jay yelled. "It's that redneck from upstate and he's got a shotgun!"

Jay fumbled with the tiny pistol in his pocket as the redneck—what was his name? Edgar?—raised the shotgun and let go a blast. He felt the pellets whiz over his head, didn't have time to look and see if Kay had gotten out of the way.

He managed to get the itty-bitty gun clear of his pocket, for whatever good it was gonna do. He came up on one knee, snapped the baby gun up, pointed it through the shattered window in Edgar's general direction, and squeezed the trigger—

There came a roar like bomb going off; a fairly new Cadillac parked across the street blew apart in a blast of fire and smoke. The recoil from the tiny pistol knocked Jay backward a good ten feet.

"Holy shit!" Jay yelled when he found his voice. His ears rang and his nostrils were filled with the smell of something acrid and sharp. He stared at the little gun.

Kay, lying flat with his hands over his neck, scrambled to his feet and pulled his gun.

In the street, the dead Caddy was nothing but a frame and burning tires. Edgar was out of sight.

Jay came up, ran after Kay.

They made it to the sidewalk, just in time to see Edgar slap the tow truck driver hard enough to knock him twenty feet through the air. Dude had a mean punch.

Edgar leaped into the tow truck and hit the gas.

"Shit!" Kay yelled. He lowered his weapon.

A crowd of seen-it-all pedestrians thought this drama was worthy enough to stop and stare at.

The tow truck and Zap-Em van was moving but not too fast. Jay lined up with the Noisy Cricket. Closed one eye, to see the rudimentary sights better . . .

"Don't—" Kay began.

Jay braced himself, held the tiny gun two-handed. Fired—

Despite his braced stance the gun's recoil knocked him down again. Damn!

The shot hit the tow truck's tow arm, blew it off. The tow truck and Zap-Em van separated. The tow truck sped up.

The Zap-Em truck rolled into a parked Thunderbird and did some major damage before it stopped.

Jay jumped up, ran to get a better angle on the fleeing Edgar.

"Jay! Not in front of the civilians!"

Jay ignored him, jumped on top of a car, lined up on the tow truck, squeezed the trigger—

—just as a moving van pulled in front of the tow truck, blocking it.

The moving van exploded, showered furniture in all directions. A couch flew past, a dining-room table and chairs, a bookcase. The crowd of civilians scattered to avoid the debris.

Jay was blown backward through the window of a car parked behind him. His butt ended up nearly in the face of the panicked woman driver. By the time he struggled free, Edgar was gone.

Kay came over, grabbed Jay by one arm, led him away from the pedestrians. Said, "We don't discharge these weapons in front of civilians."

" 'Noisy Cricket,' huh? Very funny. Ho, ho, ho." Jay looked at the tiny gun.

"Come on, we've got to get a containment team here—"

"Can we drop the cover-up bullshit, Kay? I mean, what's a couple of cars and trucks when we got an alien battle cruiser about to blow us away if we don't—"

"Listen up, Sparky, there is *always* an alien battle cruiser or a Korlian death ray or some intergalactic plague about to wipe out life on this planet. We stop it. We've *always* stopped it, and I don't plan on screwing up this time. The only thing that allows people here to get on with their lives is that *they don't know about it*! How do you think they would feel if they knew? There'd be a panic that would trash half the planet and cause thousands, maybe millions of deaths!"

Jay thought about it a second. Yeah, Kay was right. He looked at the crowd of horrified and puzzled on-lookers. Yeah, it was like that Jack Nicholson line about handling the truth. Maybe it was better they didn't re-member any of this. "Just a little swamp gas, folks. Nothing to worry about."

He looked at Kay. "But he got away."

"He won't leave town," Kay said.

"How do you know?"

"Look at the Zap-Em truck. That thing covered up in the back? That's his ship."

Kay pulled his cell phone. "Zed? We're gonna need a class-one containment team down here at the jewelry store ASAP. We spotted the bug. No, he got away, but we got his ride. Uh-huh. Right."

Kay shut the cell phone off, looked at Jay.

"What?"

"We'll stay here until the team arrives to clean up and collect the ship. Then we're going back to HQ."

Jay shook his head. Despite the black suit and ugly car, this job sure wasn't boring. Could sure say that.

Kay looked at the screen and watched several of the identifying lights blink out even as he stood there. He and the kid headed for Zed's office.

When they got there, Zed looked up at Kay and shook his head. "Containment might be a moot point. Way they are leaving, there's probably a sign at the port that says, 'Will the last extee boarding ship please turn off the lights?' "

"It can't be that bad," Jay said. "Can it?"

Zed stood, went to the door, pointed to the floor below. Said, "We've got *staff* leaving."

Kay looked, saw three Vermars carrying suitcases. "Damn. I can't believe Iggy is bailing. I thought he was a stand-up worm."

He realized when he said it the kid would probably make some wisecrack about that, but it must have slipped past.

"They all have more experience with bugs

16

than we do," Zed said. "This is like a big family dinner at an expensive restaurant. Nobody wants to wait around and get stuck with the check."

"What about the Arquillians?" Kay said.

"Apparently we're still having having some problems with the Arquillian cross-dictionary in our translator. We've only gotten part of the message so far. Says, 'Deliver the galaxy.'

"Great. Wonderful. Nobody knows what the hell is going on."

"You see?" Jay said. "I told you it had something to do with a galaxy. Maybe they want a Ford, you know, like you drive. Ford Galaxy?"

Kay impaled Jay with a stare. The kid grinned. He had cojones of pure brass, no question.

"It gets better," Zed continued. He called to the twins. "Put the deep shot onscreen, would you please?"

At least the twins hadn't left yet.

The big screen's image shifted.

Zed said, "And another contestant has entered the ring. . . ."

"Uh-oh," Kay said.

He looked at the scale. There was a second battle cruiser, only a few thousand miles away from the Arquillians.

"Lemme guess," Jay said. "The little green dude's family. They're pissed at us too?"

"Baltian battlewagon, that's right. Give the man a cigar."

"You looking to give me lung cancer?"

"You won't have time to develop it. In fact, you won't have time to *smoke* it, we don't get our asses in gear and fix this situation."

"Just how are we gonna do that?"

"What we need is a better understanding of galactic politics. There's stuff going on here with the B's and A's we don't know about, we need some background."

"Is there like, an encyclopedia? Like an outer-internet or something?"

"That's the problem with you young guys, you think can learn everything off a video or computer. No, what we need is an expert. I know just the guy—if he hasn't skipped the planet yet."

"I'm with you, chief. Lead on."

"Go," Zed said. "Time is running out."

Kay nodded. "You heard the man. Let's roll."

They headed out.

Edgar drove the tow vehicle to a stop, exited, and cursed under his breath as he walked away from it. Terran police and military were not supposed to have weaponry like that used against him at the bauble shop. This meant that the local border patrol was aware of him. They would be on the watch for this vehicle. Worse, they now had his ship.

What to do? He had to get control of this situation! He had to find that which he sought and he had to find it *soon!* Without that, the ship was the least of his worries. He wasn't leaving this rock without what he came for. By now, either the Baltians or the Arquillians—or both—should have a naval vessel in the neighborhood. When they found out about their dead ambassadors, they were going to be more than a bit irate. That part was going according to plan, but after that, things had completely fallen apart.

Well, no, not completely. He was sure he knew where

the prize was—just not exactly where it was. But he could find it if he had a small bit of information. He had circled back to the eatery where he'd killed the two ambassadors and watched from hiding briefly before he left with the box the Baltian had carried. Saw what had transpired as the bodies were removed. Knew where the prize had to have been taken.

He arrived in the vicinity of a small structure, upon which were a number of printed periodicals. Ah, yes, an information building, called a newsstand. The human behind the counter stared at him.

Edgar considered his situation. Well, all right. This *was* an information kiosk, was it not? Edgar moved quickly, caught the human by his upper body clothing, lifted his feet clear of the ground. "Where do you keep your dead?"

"I—I—I don't have any dead!" the human blurted out.

Edgar shook him, heard his teeth clack together. And something that rattled. Probably his tiny brain inside that ugly skull.

"Try again, fleshboy. Where are the dead kept?"

"I dunno! The city morgue?"

He tossed the vendor away to crash into the kiosk's back wall. As he started to leave, he caught sight of a display of rectangular cards, upon which were pictures of various buildings. Landmarks of New York City, said the caption over the display. Postcards, $1 Each. One of the images in particular drew his attention. Ah. He grabbed the card, started to walk away.

"You owe me a buck, pal!" the vendor yelled after him.

Edgar ignored the entreaty.

Now—how to find the city morgue?

Kay's driving now made a cabdriver on speed look like a little old man with a hat on going for a Sunday cruise. He leaned on the car's horn, passed in the wrong-way lanes, even went up on the sidewalk at one point, scaring the crap out of a wino in a doorway. Wino had been a hair slower, they'd have rolled over both his feet.

Or, if the wino was an alien, maybe his pseudopods. Or tentacle. Or fins.

"Take it easy, man."

"No time," Kay said.

Finally, they pulled to a screeching stop outside a kiosk. Orchard Street, Jay realized. A guy with a little pug dog at his feet was closing the stand. The guy wore a dirty cardigan, a watch cap, fingerless gloves, and filthy pants. His face was full of tics and twitches. "Terrible disguise," Jay said, as he and Kay bailed from the LTD. "Any fool can see this guy's an alien."

"Hey, you don't like it, you can kiss my furry little butt."

This didn't come from the guy, however.

It came from the dog.

Jay looked down.

"Meet Frank the Pug," Kay said. "How's it goin', Frank?"

"Sorry, Kay, I can't talk, I gotta go. My ride is leaving. I'm cutting it close as it is."

Kay bent, grabbed the dog. It yelped like, well, like a dog. "Hey! Lemme go!"

"Can't, Frank. I need some information."

"This is illegal!" the pug said.

"File a complaint with your ambassador—if you can find him. My bet is he's already lifted himself."

"Come on, Kay, leggo. You can't do this."

"Call the pound, Jay. We got us a stray. Ready to be locked up for a few days, Frank? We'll put Fido here on ice so he can't spring you."

"You can't do this! Get your paws offa me!"

A couple of pedestrians slowed to glare at Kay. You could mug a nun on Fifth Avenue during rush hour and nobody would stop to help, but if you mistreated a dog, book it, a lynch mob would quickly form to string you up. Jay remembered seeing a news clip once of some natural disaster in South America or Central America, an earthquake. All these peons sitting outside their knocked-down shacks, had no food, no water, no place to sleep but out in the rain. Old grannies, women with babies. There had been a mama dog with a couple of puppies in the back of the scene. The TV station got thousands of letters offering to help.

Most of the letters were offering to help the dogs.

Well, he could understand that. More he learned about people, the better dogs looked to him. They'd had a dog when he lived at home with his folks, and no matter what trouble he might be in with his parents, the dog was always happy to see him come through the door. Skipped school? Forgot to mow the lawn? Dented the car's fender? Hey, Lena didn't care. Go outside to get the mail and bring it in, and there was Lena, jumping up and down, grinning, licking his hand, and you could almost hear her thinking: "He's back! He's back! Hurray! Joy!" The cat never cared if he lived or died long as he got fed, but the dog loved him no matter what. Something to be said for that kind of companionship.

The fake pug growled, tried a few yips. He must have

known how people were about dogs, too. People slowed. Did somebody say, Get a rope?

Jay said, "No problem here, folks. The dog is, ah, helping us in an investigation."

"Arquillians and Baltians," Kay said. "What do you know?"

"Kay, I really don't have time for this."

"Sooner you tell me, sooner you can be on your way."

"Okay, okay. The A's and B's are from different galaxies, have been fighting since forever. Mostly over rule of a third galaxy. There was a peace conference downtown somewhere, the B's were gonna turn the galaxy over to the A's, or vice versa, I dunno, and sign a treaty. The bug had other ideas. You know how bugs are, Kay."

Kay looked at Jay, who didn't have a clue. "The bug's colony has been living off this war for centuries."

Jay said, "What about the belt?"

"Yeah. Rosenberg said something about Orion's belt before he croaked," Kay said to the pug. "What did he mean?"

Somebody on the walk stopped, said, "Are you mistreating that dog, buddy?"

Jay glanced at the guy, who looked like he might have been a Russian weightlifter, in the supermonster class. "Nope, no problem. Dog's gotta go to the vet, he hates it. Got worms."

The weightlifter looked dubious, but he moved on.

Frank the Pug said, "Beats me. I heard the galaxy was here, on the planet."

"Here?" Kay said.

"Millions and millions of stars and planets and shit? Here? I don't get it," Jay added.

The dog smirked. "You humans, you don't get much of anything. When are you gonna learn that size doesn't matter? Just because something is important, doesn't mean it's got to be big. The galaxy in question is tiny by local standards. Very small."

"How small?" Kay asked.

"I dunno exactly. Maybe as big as a marble. Or a jewel."

"Jesus," Jay said.

"Okay, Kay, that's it, that's all I know. Now, if you'll put me down, I need to be walked before the flight."

Kay put the pug down. The dog said, "Good luck, Kay. I don't think you've got a prayer, but I'll be rooting for you. I like it here. Lotta fire hydrants in a city this size."

The pug and his human—who didn't seem the least disturbed that the dog could talk—left.

Jay said, "Maybe he didn't mean 'belt.' "

Kay frowned at him. "What?"

"The little green dude. His English was bad, he had to struggle for the words. Maybe he didn't mean 'belt.' Maybe he meant something else."

"What?"

It dawned on them at about the same time.

"Get in the car," Kay said.

Jay was already on the way.

Inside, Jay said, "Okay, lemme see if I can get this straight. The Arquillians are from one galaxy, the Baltians are from another and they are fighting over a *third* galaxy, which is about the size of a marble."

"That seems to be the situation," Kay said.

"Okay. And the bugs want to make sure that the fighting continues, so our boy Edgar is here to screw the peace treaty up."

"Which he has had some success at doing thus far, yes."

Jay stared at a pedestrian trying to cross the street. Kay ran the light and nearly ran the guy down. The pedestrian gestured wildly at the LTD as it roared past, not slowing in the least.

Jay said, "I still don't get it. Why doesn't Zed just send a message to the A's and B's and tell them about the bug? I mean, they must have some experience with these dudes, right?"

"Now there's a reasonable attitude," Kay said. He whipped the wheel to the left, swerved around a woman pushing a baby carriage across the street, missed hitting it by a good two inches. "Thing is," Kay continued, "these off-worlders don't altogether trust humans. They've, ah, had some bad experiences down here."

Jay looked at him. "Bad experiences?"

"Well, yes. First few years we had aliens coming to visit, I reckon the Eiffel Tower and the Brooklyn Bridge got sold to some of the more gullible tourists a few hundred times. And a whole bunch of swampland in Florida got peddled, too."

"No."

"Oh, yeah. We nearly had an all-out war when a Vulvarian businessman tried to take possession of the Chrysler Building a few years back."

"Oh, boy."

"Exactly. So we don't have the reputation of galactic Boy Scouts down here when it comes to being trustworthy, loyal, and helpful and all like that. That's not even counting the muggers, street gangs, prostitutes, and others who prey on tourists. We could tell the captains of those battle cruisers up here that a bug was responsible for the deaths of their prince and ambassador and they would smile and nod as they warmed up their planet-buster guns."

"Soddit," Jay said.

"Excuse me?"

"Some other dude did it. Heard that a lot on the job. Perps would say, 'Hey, you wrong, Jack, I couldn'ta done it, I was in De-troit at the time.'"

"Then you see the problem here."

"Yeah. We got to catch the bug, get the galaxy from him, and do some fast talking."

"If Edgar has the galaxy."

"Huh?"

Kay glanced over at him, almost ran over a traffic cop. The cop blew his whistle and started to write down the car's license number. Knowing how it worked when you were on the street, Jay figured the guy wasn't going to report it, but get the owner's home address from the DMV and show up later to flatten a few tires or maybe key the paint. Though on this car, he probably wouldn't bother trying to disfigure it. Who would care?

Kay said, "Why do you figure he was at the jewelry store? Looking for a nice engagement ring?"

Jay nodded. "I see what you mean. If he'da scored the galaxy, he'da been long gone by now." He paused a second. "Maybe he didn't figure out what we did. Maybe he doesn't have a clue to where it is."

Kay shook his head. "Can't bet on that, hoss. He was in the store before we were, he saw the same things we saw. The bugs aren't stupid. Only thing we can hope is that we beat him to it."

"What you dragging ass along for, then? Why don't you step on it?"

Kay nodded.

He stepped on it.

. . .

Laurel Weaver, Deputy Medical Examiner for the City of New York, stood over the corpse of a guy dug up from a shallow and secluded spot in Central Park. The body, with multiple gunshot wounds to the head, face, and body, had been uncovered by a pair of persistent toy poodles who had slipped their leashes. When their owner, a blue-haired woman of seventy, had caught up with them, the dogs had managed to dig down to one arm and were chewing on the fingers. There was no ID, but the body was fresh, only a day or so old, and finger-prints revealed the body to be that of one Arnold A. Cohen, a former Wall Street financier who had cost his clients millions when the junk bond market collapsed.

He'd been indicted but had jumped bail and disap-peared before his trial.

Laurel had removed sixteen bullets so far, and as nearly as she could tell, the slugs were of at least four different calibers—.38, 9mm, .22, and .45. It might be premature, but her guess was that several of the late Mr. Cohen's investors had caught up with him. Either that, or maybe he was killed by a gun collector who wanted to use a lot of hardware just for the fun of it. Maybe a guy who used guns owned by different relatives who had lost money because of Mr. Cohen? Here, *bam!* that's for Aunt Sarah! And *bang! bang!* this is for Uncle Louie! And *ka-pow!* Granny Klein sends her love!

She frowned. What a weird train of thought. She felt kind of spaced out today. The day was normal, nothing out of the ordinary, but she kept fuzzing, kept finding herself daydreaming. Remembering things that had hap-pened to her as a child. It was as if her brain wasn't working quite right, it kept skipping around like an old, scratched phonograph record.

Well. She'd been working pretty hard lately. Maybe she needed a vacation.

She turned her attention back to Mr. Cohen. Found a new caliber, looked to be a .25.

Could this guy have gotten blasted by five different people?

Boy, this was like an Agatha Christie novel. . . .

Edgar found a mechanical signaling device upon the counter inside the morgue. He slammed his hand down upon the small rod extending from the metal hemisphere and was rewarded with a sharp ringing tone. He repeated his action several times.

He noted as he rang the bell that the disguise's terminal appendage—the hand—was beginning to look somewhat the worse for wear. The skin had taken on a grayish color and thin sheets of the integument had peeled away from the underlying flesh.

If he didn't get this business attended to quickly, he was most assuredly going to have to find a new disguise. That alone was worth a large amount of increased speed.

A human came forth from inside of a small security cage. He carried with him a compact

17

print-on-paper reader—a book—upon whose cover were the words *Atlas Shrugged*. He also carried a device whose function Edgar could not immediately determine. It appeared to be a thin, flat, hand-sized rectangle of flexible slotted plastic attached to a thin rod about as long as the human's forearm. Some kind of fan? A signaling device?

Upon his breast, the human wore an ID tag that read, "Tony."

The Tony said, "Thank you so much for making sure the bell still works."

A small flying creature buzzed around Edgar, drawn no doubt by the decaying disguise. The winged insectoid alighted upon the counter in front of the human. Edgar smiled at it.

Quickly, the human used the fanlike device, slapped it down upon the hapless insectoid with a snappy motion.

This move crushed the insectoid more or less flat, splattering bits of it here and there.

"Gotcha!" the human said. He raised the swatting device and used the edge of it to scrape the dead insectoid from the counter. He flapped the thing and the smashed creature fell upon the floor. "What can I do for you, Farmer John? Aside from get you some soap? You have a real problem with B.O., friend." The speaker wrinkled its nose.

Another time he would have punished the Tony, but, he reminded himself, he *was* in a hurry. "A human came in here earlier. A dead man."

The creature rolled its disgusting eyes in its bony sockets. "Imagine that! A dead man at the morgue! And this means what to me?"

Edgar effected a smile, no easy task. "The dead man was a dear friend of mine. He had an animal with him, a pet . . . cat. It was a gift I gave him and since he is now dead, I would like it back."

"Uh-huh, sure, I can understand that. No problem. Thing is, I'll need a picture ID, written proof of ownership of the cat, or notarized proof of kinship with the deceased—"

The human used the swatter again, crushed another of the small insectoids who chanced to land upon the counter near the site where his brother had been slain moments earlier.

"Don't do that," Edgar said. He strived to maintain the benign expression.

"Do what?" the man said. He snapped the swatter, killed another brother. "You a vegetarian or something?"

Edgar put his hands upon the counter. Several of the larger insectoids who had hitched a ride under his clothes chose that moment to depart.

"Shit! You got roaches!"

The morgue human ducked under the counter, came up with a metal cylinder. Upon the can was a picture of a dying insectoid and the word "Raid" in large, colorful letters.

Edgar let the smile go and replaced it with a frown.

The Tony pointed the cylinder at the small brothers and put his finger upon a small plastic control atop the device.

"I don't think so," Edgar said.

Kay pulled the LTD to a stop. Jay said, "How about I handle this one? You wait out here."

Kay stared at him. "Excuse me? Why the hell should I?"

"Because all we need is the cat. I can walk in there, get it, be back in five minutes. If *you* go in, you're gonna lay your Jack Webb on the Doc, flash her with your brain ray, and maybe give her leukemia or some shit. The woman is a doctor, she doesn't need you erasing half of her medical school education."

Kay grinned. "You like her. Okay. Five minutes."

Jay nodded.

Edgar grabbed the female human and tossed her across the room. She slammed into the wall, slid down it, stunned. He moved to stand over her.

"Where is it? The animal?"

The female shook her head. "I told you, I don't know. It ran under a gurney or something, over there!"

"Best you find it!" He grabbed her, lifted her, carried her in the direction to which she'd been pointing.

The female said, "Here, kitty, kitty. Here Orion, here, baby!"

"Orion?"

"The name on its collar," she said. "C'mon, kitty—"

There was a blurry streak as the animal ran out past them. It was fast for a furred animal. It ran across the room, leaped up onto a storage cabinet, climbed higher on another cabinet and disappeared.

Edgar growled. He started to turn that way.

The bell at the front entrance rang.

"Hello?" a human voice called. "Anybody home?"

Edgar recognized the tone. One of the border patrol humans who had fired upon him at the bauble place. Undoubtedly armed and looking for him! No room to maneuver in here, he'd be a sitting glurk.

He stared at the human female. "Do you wish to continue living?"

"Yes."

"Then do exactly as I say."

Laurel had thought the client with eighteen bullets in five different calibers was the most unusual thing she had seen in a while but this guy took the prize. Unless her nose had suddenly malfunctioned, he smelled like he was dead. And a quick look at him, well, you didn't have to be a board-certified dermatologist to know this guy had some serious skin disease. He was blotchy, gray, and peeling like somebody who fell asleep on the beach in August without applying any sunblock. And he looked like the saggy-baggy elephant, he had wrinkles on his neck and arms where she'd never seen wrinkles on any-body under a hundred.

But whoever he was, he was as strong as a gorilla and dangerous. She had no desire to join her customers on a table. She hoped whoever it was coming in the door was somebody who could get her out of this before Bozo killed her.

A good-looking young black guy came into the room. He looked familiar, but Laurel couldn't place where she'd seen him before.

Jay had seen that the door behind the counter and secu-rity cage was open. He headed that way.

He found the exam room. There was Laurel. She stood next to an exam table, no body on it, just a sheet draped over it, all the way to the floor. Just stood there like she had forgotten who she was. Maybe that damned brain scrambler had done something to her?

There was the body of a middle-aged white male on the table behind her. Looked like it had been shot up pretty good.

"Hi," Jay said.

"Hello," Laurel said. Her voice definitely sounded funny. He was going to have words with Kay about this if her mind was messed up. And he had to remember that she didn't remember him, so he was a blank.

Well. He could certainly do a cop. Could probably even use his own real name, but there wasn't any point in maybe muddying those waters. So he said, "I'm, uh, Sergeant Preston, from the Twenty-sixth Precinct. They brought a cat in here with a corpse, might have said Orion on the name tag?"

"Yes. That's right. A cat. A very popular cat."

"Right. Well, the cat is, um, a witness in a murder case. I'm going to need to take it with me."

"Ah, I, uh, don't know where the cat is right at the moment," she said. She shrugged.

"You don't?"

"No."

She lowered her voice to a whisper: "Maybe you could take me with you instead?"

"Excuse me?"

"I said, 'Maybe you could take me with you instead.' "

Jay grinned. "Man, you work fast, don't you?"

Her face got serious and the whisper was nearly a hiss: "Listen. I'd really like to go with you *now!*"

Jay grinned. Hey, change the name, change the clothes, he still had it. The old charm shined through.

161

Good Lord, Laurel thought. This dope thinks I'm coming on to him! If he's a cop, he's got to have a gun under that ugly black suit and I need to figure out a way to wake him up!

Without giving it away what I'm doing. Subtle. Keep it subtle.

Kay stepped out of the car, set the alarm, and headed into the building. The kid was trying to do the right thing, but he couldn't wait all day. When the fate of Earth, not to mention a galaxy or three was at stake, there wasn't time to screw around.

Kay found his way to the morgue's front desk. The attendant was not evident, probably on the phone or something. All right, he'd give the kid another couple minutes. Besides, he really needed a smoke. Kay pulled a cigarette from his pack, leaned against the counter, hunted for a light. What the hell, if the world was gonna go up, one more wouldn't hurt, right? He had a pack of matches somewhere . . .

"I'd *really* like to go with you, *now*," Laurel said.

"Yeah? Why is that?" He grinned.

She didn't return the smile. "Can we go?" She looked down at her waist. Said, "I have something I need to show you."

Jay raised his eyebrows. "Slow down there, sweetie. No hurry. You don't have to hit the gas like that. I'm with you."

She leaned toward him, lowered her voice even more.

Her face was tense. Lust, maybe? She said, "You don't understand. You really need to see this."

He nodded. "I hear that. And I look forward to it, believe me. But let's just get something straight here, okay? I'm not into some kind of macho trip or anything, but I kinda like to do the driving myself, you understand?"

How could she have thought this guy was attractive? He was obviously a moron. What did she have to do, draw him a picture? Kick him in the shins? Men! They all thought they were God's gift to women, every one of them.

She had to wrap this up and wrap it up now. No more time for subtle. Cut to the chase, girl. He's a cop, he ought to know how to deal with bad guys, right?

Kay struck a match to light his cigarette. The match sizzled and went out. He frowned at it, dropped the dead match, reached for another one. . . .

Laurel bared her teeth at him in something that definitely was *not* a smile. "Listen up, *stud,* I know your brains aren't in gear, but there is *something* you have to help me with!" She pointed at the examination table.

Jay grinned. Right here? On the table? Man.

Fool! she thought. Dolt! Ignoramus! Idiot! Pinhead! She wanted to slap him.

And yet, even so, she couldn't shake the feeling she knew him from somewhere. And that he really was cute. Maybe he had hidden talents. Surely he must have.

"Under-hey ee-they able-tay," she whispered in pig latin.

Jay had always been pretty good at pig latin. Under-hey, that was "under." Ee-they, that was "the." Able-tay . . .

Under the table?

Oh, *shit.*

Now he got it. She wasn't coming on to him.

She was *warning* him.

He pulled the little gun he'd been issued—

Finally! The cop got it!

But—what was that tiny little gun in his hand? Laurel frowned. Since when did NYPD start issuing derringers—?

As Kay lifted the second match, it also went out. He frowned at it, saw there was a blob of something gooey on the match. Where had that come from—?

He looked up.

A dead man was stuck to the high ceiling by a wad of viscous, dripping goo. The guy had a can of Raid in one hand and a really surprised expression on his face.

Shit! You didn't need to be a weatherman to know which way *that* wind blew! Edgar! He'd beaten them here!

Kay pulled his Series Four and sprinted for the door behind the counter—

The morgue table came up like a bomb went off under it and there was Edgar. Jay whipped the Cricket around, but Edgar grabbed Laurel and shoved the barrel of a shotgun under her chin, just as Kay ran into the room waving his deatomizer.

"Freeze right there, bug!" Kay yelled. He had his weapon aimed at Edgar, held tight in both hands, not wavering the slightest.

"Don't shoot! Don't shoot!" Jay yelled. He kept his gun pointed at Edgar but knew he didn't have a clear target, even this close. Especially since he didn't know what the Cricket would do at any range.

"Christ, you're thick," Laurel said to Jay.

"Sorry. How was I supposed to know?"

"What did I have to do, *sing* it for you? 'There's a psych-o-path under the table'?"

"Maybe if you'd tried something other than a street hooker routine—"

"So typical of a man! Let a woman show any sign of independence and they don't know what to do. I can't believe I thought you were cute."

"You thought I was cute?"

"I hate to interrupt your mating ritual, but put the weapons down!" Edgar said.

"Not gonna happen, insect," Kay said. "Put *yours* down."

Edgar started to back away, dragging Laurel with him.

"Let her go," Kay said.

"So you can deatomize me? I don't think so. You can't hit me without killing her."

Edgar kept shuffling backward. He moved into the hall, then toward the end of the corridor. There was a chicken-wire window there, but it was painted shut.

Kay and Jay followed Edgar and Laurel into the hall.

"Stay back," Edgar said. "I'll kill her."

"If you do that, I will surely kill you," Kay said. "You know I can't let you go, even if we have to lose a civilian."

"Lose a civilian?" Laurel said. "Are we talking about *me* here?"

"It's okay, Laurel," Jay said.

"Really? How do you figure that, goat-boy?" she said. She glanced quickly toward Edgar, then down at the shotgun.

"I mean, it will be okay. We'll work something out."

"Don't bet on it, meat sack," Edgar said.

"Last chance. Let her go, shit eater," Kay said. He lined up on Edgar's face with his weapon.

"Dung! Not shit, *dung*. And listen up, monkey-boy, I might have to take that at my end of the galaxy but compared to you, I'm on the top rung of the evolutionary ladder, so just shut the greb up with that kind of talk."

At that moment, Orion the cat decided to put in his—or was it her?—two cents' worth. The cat scrabbled out of nowhere, launched itself at Edgar, a hissing mass of claws and teeth. The cat landed on the alien's head and slashed and bit. Edgar let got of Laurel and whipped his free hand up, pulled the cat free. Saw the little dangling bell on the cat's collar and grinned.

Kay was right, he wasn't stupid.

Edgar grabbed the bell, jerked it free, and tossed the

cat, all with the same fast hand, never moved the shotgun from under Laurel's chin. He put the bell into his mouth and swallowed it, then grinned.

"Damn," Kay said. "I'm sorry, lady, but I got no choice."

He extended his weapon. . . .

Jay yelled, "Kay, don't—!"

With that, Edgar and Laurel just sort of *flew* toward the window. Crashed right through it as Kay fired and the whole end of the corridor rippled and vanished with a terrific roar.

When the dust cleared, Jay ran to the hole where the wall had been. There was an air shaft beyond the hole, leading up and down. Jay looked both ways into the shaft. No sign of them.

He looked at Kay, then at the gun Kay held. "Did that thing—are they—?"

Kay leaned into the shaft. "No. I missed. Come on!"

The two of them headed for the entrance.

This was bad. Very bad.

This was definitely *not* going the way Edgar had envisioned. Being shot at by fleshboys with decent weapons was not generally a good thing.

His ship was captured; by now the off-worlder ships would be warming up the planetbusters in preparations for their battle. There were border patrol agents actively seeking him and they had the cutting edge of whatever technology had come to this world from other planets.

No, none of these things were good things.

On the other pincher, he *did* have the prize. He also had a hostage that seemed to have some value—not much, given the deatomizer blast one of the meat sacks had let go at him—and he had a head start.

True, his ship was inaccessible, but it was a piece of junk likely to blow up on takeoff any-how, so it wasn't such a great loss. There were

18

other ways to leave this dirt ball. And he had one of such ways in mind.

"Where are we going?" the human female yelled.

"Shut up," Edgar said. He had her under one arm and while she wasn't that heavy, it was a bit awkward carrying her like that. *Where* they were going in the near future was not a problem. How they would *get* there was another thing altogether. Especially considering that Edgar did not know the whereabouts of the location he needed, nor the way to proceed, had he known. Something of a problem; however, having obtained a local guide when capturing the female ought to solve that part of the problem.

Once outside the building and on the street, transportation could be arranged.

They achieved the paved pathway. Edgar stepped out into the street and in front of one of the for-hire vehicles called a "cab."

The vehicle screeched to a stop a feeler's thickness away from Edgar and the human female.

Naturally, the pilot of the craft leaned out of his window, made the universal hand gesture of greeting, and began yelling.

Edgar's translator was a top-of-the-line model, with more than two hundred terran dialects programmed into it, but it was unable to recognize whatever language the pilot spewed in his direction. How ever did these humans communicate with one another?

Edgar moved toward the pilot, dragging the human female along.

The pilot screamed something that sounded like, "Bong-ong-fong-gong-spong your momma!"

No time, no time! The fleshboys would be out looking for a target any second. Edgar reached into the vehicle, grabbed the pilot, and jerked him through the open window. He tossed the driver away, then remembered to open the door. He jumped into the craft, pulled the female in behind him. "I am unfamiliar with the local pathways," he said. "You shall operate the vehicle. Take us to this location."

He held out the postcard with the picture upon it, the one he had taken from the information kiosk earlier.

"Huh?"

"Take us to this location. Immediately."

"What?"

No time, no time! He flashed his triple row of serrated fangs at her from within the disguise, stretching the face somewhat to do so.

She screamed.

Blast! Edgar engaged the gear mechanism of the craft and simultaneously pressed his foot against the acceleration pedal. The vehicle lunged forward and the female grabbed at the directional control wheel.

"All right, all right, I got it, I got it!" she said.

"You know the location of which I am desirous?"

"Yeah, yeah."

"Good. Obey local vehicular regulations and proceed there at the utmost legal speed."

The former occupant of the vehicle ran behind them, waving his hands and continuing to utter what surely must be curses, in whatever language it was in which he was fluent. Edgar turned and waved at him with the universal gesture. It meant so many things, the finger signal: hello, good-bye, acknowledgment, irritation. One of the few things he'd seen on this planet that seemed useful.

Well, This wasn't so bad, all things considered. He was alive, he had the galaxy, he was escaping pursuit.

Things could surely be worse. He leaned back and looked at the female. Ugly creature. How could any male of any species possibly find such a—a *monster* like her sexually attractive? Perhaps she had some redeeming characteristic, some hidden olfactory or other signal to draw in a male? You must have to be human to see it, for certainly Edgar could not. It was hard enough telling the males from the females, much less the differences between those of the same sex.

They all looked alike to Edgar.

Of course, this one *was* a keeper of the dead, a relatively exalted position where he came from; being able to dispense corpse food was, after all, a position of some power.

Laurel knew she was in big trouble when the psycho crashed through the window at the office carrying her, landed safely, then bounded out onto the street as easily as a man hopping around on the moon.

This was, she realized, no ordinary psycho.

When he—no, when *it* whipped that cabbie out of the cab one-handed and threw him like he was an empty Coke can, that was another clue. Okay, to that point, you might make the case that the guy was *hopped up* on some kind of drugs. Steroids, speed, angel dust, and that was how he did such stuff. Unlikely, sure, but possible.

But when he flashed what looked like three sets of shark fangs from within a mouth that could not—absolutely *could not*—be inside a human being's head, she knew for absolutely certain that the thing sitting next to her and telling her to drive was not human.

And that cop—if that's what he was—and that man

with the big gun had known it, too. *Bug,* the white guy had called it.

It sure as hell didn't look like any bug she'd ever seen. What had she gotten into the middle of? This was so incredible she couldn't begin to get a handle on it.

"We are proceeding in the proper direction?" the thing asked.

"Yeah, yeah," she said.

"Continue," it said.

Laurel maybe wasn't the smartest woman on the planet but she was not stupid. She put two and two together and figured out that this monster next to her was not of this world. It didn't look right, it didn't act right, it didn't talk right. It wasn't human, not with that physiology, and she didn't think there were any other intelligent species native to Earth, the Yeti and Sasquatch notwithstanding.

Ergo, this creature was not from around here.

An alien.

A little green man. Except not so little and my, what big teeth it had, Grandma.

She was being kidnapped by an alien and forced to drive to, to—

She felt a sudden urge to laugh, but she managed to keep from doing it. Once she got started down that road, she might not be able to stop. She knew all about hysteria and she wasn't far from that state. But—really.

She was being *kidnapped by an alien*.

It was right off the front page of one of those sleazy tabloids!

Nobody at the office was going to believe this one. Assuming she survived to tell them.

But—if it had wanted her dead, wouldn't it have killed her by now?

Not if it needs a driver, her little internal voice chirped at her. *And maybe he has other plans for you. Remember those headlines: ALIEN FATHERED MY BABY. And all those . . .* probe *things that always seemed to happen?*

Great. That's all I needed to hear.

She looked at the alien. Its skin was peeling, flaky, and didn't seem to fit right. Definitely something wrong with this picture. If she had noticed it before, she could have maybe gotten away.

No point in dwelling on the road not taken.

And what had it wanted with that cat? She'd seen it rip the animal's collar off, or at least the little bell— which hadn't worked, she'd never heard it ring. What was that all about?

Never mind that. Take it to where it wants to go. When it gets out, floor the pedal and get the hell away from it.

It was not much of a plan, but it was as good as she could come up with at the moment.

"They're in a cab!" Jay yelled.

"How do you figure that?"

Jay waved at the man standing in the middle of the street screaming in some unknown language. "Got to be a cabdriver."

Jay ran toward a line of cabs gridlocked at the intersection ahead. He pounded on windows, yelling, "Laurel! Laurel!"

Scared the shit out of a couple of people, must be tourists. The locals paid him no mind, went on about reading their papers or whatever else people normally did in the back of cabs.

He was fifteen cabs up the way when a horn honked behind him. He didn't even look up.

"You're wasting time," Kay yelled.

Jay turned, saw Kay in the LTD.

"Get in. He won't be leaving the planet in a cab."

"What?"

"We have his ship. Get in."

Back at HQ, things were a lot quieter than Jay had seen them so far. A lot of the aliens weren't there, although the twins were still hanging in.

Zed saw Kay and Jay, waved them over.

"The two warships are still up there," he said. He waved at the big screen. "Each of them thinks the other killed his guy and each of them thinks the other has the galaxy, as far as we can tell."

"Each of them seems to think we're in league with the other, too."

"Swell. Edgar's got it. The bug," Jay said.

"We had him, but lost him," Kay said. "And now he's got the galaxy and a hostage, the medical examiner." Kay sighed. "I'm getting old, Zed. I should have taken him."

"We're all getting old, except for Speedy here." He nodded at Jay. "You don't really think he'll come here?"

Kay said, "We've got his ship in the big storage bay in this building. By now, I'd guess every pilot of any ship with star leap capability for ten light-years knows there's a bug on Earth. I'd expect they'll be screening off-world passengers real carefully."

Zed nodded. "I expect you're right."

"You've got guards posted on the ship?" Jay asked.

"Of course. I can't imagine the bug would be so stupid as to try and waltz in here, thinking he was just going to collect his ride and leave."

"He's got a hostage," Jay reminded Zed.

The older man looked at him. "Son, if that bug gets off-world with what the A's and B's want, this whole planet is apt to go up like a barbecue grill with a can of charcoal lighter sprayed on it. If any of our people get lined up on the bug, they are going to cut him down to prevent that, wouldn't matter if the hostage was Mother Theresa."

"You'd do that? Even if Laurel was in the way?"

Kay and Zed exchanged glances.

Kay looked at him. "We would. And you would, too, Jay."

Jay thought about it for a second. You tried not to negotiate with terrorists and even though he had a personal feeling for Laurel, getting every living creature on the planet killed for her would be just too lopsided an equation.

Yeah. He guessed he would have to shoot.

"So—what do we do now?" Jay asked.

Kay said, "Come on."

Kay led Jay to a command center. "Let's instigate a bio-net at all tunnels, bridges, and toll booths," he said to the tech sitting there. "Ferries, too. Scramble the airport and train squads. If it's not human, I don't want it leaving the island."

"If it's not too late," Jay said.

"If it's not too late," Kay echoed.

"Isn't there anything we can tell the guys in the warships?"

Kay shook his head. "Zed will have been trying. They don't trust us, don't much like us, wouldn't think twice about blasting us and good riddance, if they had a good enough reason. We come up with the galaxy and the bug who killed their people, do a fast song and dance, we survive. Otherwise . . ."

Jay had a vivid image of his father squeezing a can of charcoal lighter onto a smoldering barbecue when Jay had been a boy. Of the burst of flame that blew up and took his father's eyebrows and a big chunk of his hair off. Yeee.

"I can't believe they'd just destroy a whole planet like that," Jay began.

"Advanced science doesn't equal advanced mercies," Kay said. "They don't think like we do. Or maybe they do think like some of us—psycho killers or sociopaths."

"Wonderful."

"Sorry, kid, that's what makes them aliens, ain't it?"

An alarm went off, a loud, jangling siren that *whoop-whoop*ed throughout the building.

"What?! What?!"

"The Arquillians just fired a charged-particle beamer!" Zed yelled.

"At who?" Jay said.

"At us," Zed said. "Targeted on the North Sea. Tracking!"

Kay and Jay ran to where Zed stared at the big screen. The image shifted.

"Got spysat feed here," somebody said. Jay didn't see who.

There was an image of a bright laserlike beam hitting the cold ocean. Jay saw what looked like an iceberg. After a second, a cloud raised from the water.

"Superheated steam," Kay said.

"Get a wide angle," Zed ordered. "Put a scale on it!"

The image blurred. The cloud that boiled up looked

almost like an atomic mushroom. A scale down the side of the image blinked.

"Nine hundred meters tall," somebody said.

"That's not so bad, is it?" Jay said. "What's that in real numbers? I'm not good on the metric stuff."

"Little over half a mile," Kay said.

"Oh, shit."

"Exactly. And it may top about twenty times that. That's a big explosion we're looking at. They're not just cooking a few seals and whales, there's probably gonna be a tsunami slopping ashore and washing away towns from England to northwest Africa."

The alarm kept blaring. A tech yelled, "There go the Baltians!"

"Get the impact onscreen!" Zed yelled.

Another blur, and a spysat image of what looked like the middle of a sandy wasteland.

"Gobi Desert," Kay said, as a pillar of sand and flame roared skyward, nearly matching the first impact.

"Gonna be a lot of glass lying around there," somebody said.

"Maybe not for very long," Kay said. "History implies there's somebody around to remember it."

"What the hell is going on?" Jay said.

"Andromeda Convention protocols," Zed said. "They each get one free salvo, then they hunker down and try to come to terms."

Both ships fired several more beams.

"Why don't they shoot at each other instead of us?"

"Part of the rules."

"How much hunkering we talking about here?"

"About an hour, give or take," Kay said.

"And then . . . ?"

"They can't get it fixed, they start shooting. At each other, at us, at anything that they feel like blasting."

"Why can't they settle this in their own damn neighborhood?"

"Treaty requires that hostilities take place between navies only, and only in a part of the universe devoid of intelligent life."

"Devoid of intelligent life? What are we, snails?"

"From their viewpoints, pretty much. On a scale of one to a hundred, our civilization rates about a two. We get wiped out, well, it's no skin off anybody's beak."

"Sucks, but there you have it," Zed said.

Kay said, "You pull up the locations of all the land-based and orbital interstellar vehicles?"

"Yep. According to the logs, our friend Frank the Pug caught the last train out of town. I can't believe for a second anybody would be stupid enough to bring a starship here after those two opening rounds. The bug is stuck here."

"Which don't mean jackshit," Jay put in. "Except that he gets cooked with the rest of us. I'm not taking a lot of consolation from that."

"We are getting damage reports from the opening salvos," somebody said.

"Let's hear them," Zed said.

"Atlantic City is gone."

"Big loss," Kay said.

"Miami Beach, gone."

"Too bad. My favorite Cuban restaurant was there."

"Epcot is obliterated."

"Karma," Kay said.

Jay had a thought. "We still got an hour, right?"

"Hartford took a direct hit."

"What a shame," Zed said.

"Guys? If we knew where the bug went, we could still catch him!"

"Half of Paris is burning."

"Hope it's the half that thinks 'hamburger' or any American word can't be used in public. Uppity snobs."

"Guys," Jay said. "Hey, *old guys!*"

Zed and Kay turned as one to glare at him.

"Do those things still work?"

He pointed.

Zed and Kay turned to look at where Jay was pointing. On the wall in the background was the mural of the 1964 World's Fair. Prominent in the front of the picture were the two towers with the "fake" flying saucers atop them.

Zed and Kay looked at each other.

"Well, I'll be damned. Out of the mouths of babes," Zed said.

"Amen," Kay said.

Edgar looked at the postcard, then through the window of the vehicle. Yes, yes, that was the place, just ahead. Perfect!

The wording on the card said:

FLUSHING MEADOWS, SITE OF THE 1964 WORLD'S FAIR

And there, right in plain sight, two ancient Permarian saucers, each perched on top of a big post. Whatever else you could say about the nasty little creatures, they built top-of-the-line ships. The good thing was, Permarian engines and hulls were subetheric-integrated-n-dimension-interlocks, so if the hull was still intact, the engine was almost certainly operable, and from the picture—and now the direct view in the darkening day—the hulls looked just fine.

19

So who needed that crappy secondhand ship he'd been stuck with? They were welcome to it, and if they were waiting for him to come looking for it, they'd be waiting a long time. Meanwhile, he would have borrowed one of the Permarian ships and headed for points spiralward, long gone.

Well. Not so long, all things considered. The entertainment broadcaster in the cab had made mention of some sort of meteor impact on the planet, destroying some sections of it and killing a few hundred thousand of the inhabitants.

That would be the Arquillians and the Baltians flexing their muscles, Edgar knew, and no meteor impact.

Definitely time to leave this world.

"Here we are," the female said. She piloted the vehicle to a halt. "You just hop on out. I'll lock up and be right with you."

Edgar twisted the key in the ignition device and snapped it off. He exited his side of the craft.

The female rolled up the windows and locked the craft's doors.

Edgar grinned. He moved around to the female's side of the cab, grabbed the door, and jerked the door free of the craft. He grabbed the human by her arm and dragged her out with him. "Do you not enjoy my company?"

"Come on. You don't need me, whoever—whatever—you are. Why not just let me go?"

"Well, I would, but it's a long ride and I don't have time to pick up provisions."

"Meaning?"

"I might need a little snack on the way."

The female went pale. Good. Better to have her frightened and helpless. He could kill her now, hang her out a lock once they got into deep space, and flash-freeze her before going into hyperspace, but he liked his meat fresh whenever he could get it. She could probably go several days before she expired from thirst or hunger or whatever and still be a lot tastier than frozen.

One had to enjoy one's food as best one could when camping out.

"Come on." He dragged her toward a fence surrounding the area.

"This is kidnapping," she said. "We have laws! You could get the death penalty!"

"Only if your policemen catch me," Edgar said. "And from what I've seen of them so far, they can't find their xargs with both hands."

By the time they got back to the LTD, it was getting dark. Kay slid in behind the wheel and started the engine as Jay locked his seat belt into place. "Let's go bag us a bug," Kay said.

He stepped on the gas and laid rubber away from the curb.

Jay looked at a clock, then at a newscrawl on a building ticker. METS CHASE PENNANT. This followed by: RAIN LIKELY. TEMPERATURE TO DROP UNSEASONABLY LOW. This followed by: GLOBAL DISASTER AS METEOR SHOWER TURNS DEADLY.

Good that people had their priorities in order. And that meteor shower thing must be spin control by Zed or his people.

No, Jay, *our* people. You're one of them now, remember?

Kay drove in his usual maniacal way, using the gas

pedal as a brake and plenty of horn. A sudden sharp turn banged Jay's head against the window.

"Hey!"

"Sorry."

He looked up, saw a sign ahead. "Where you going? You're not taking the Midtown Tunnel?"

"Got a better way to get to Queens from here?"

"Come on, man, it'll be jammed this time of day! We'll be stuck in damned traffic when the death rays come down to roast us!"

"You know, for a young man, you worry too much."

They rolled into the tunnel. Kay weaved in and out of the lanes, passing cars and trucks like they were standing still.

Ahead of them, Jay saw the tail of the bumper-to-bumper traffic in the tunnel, new cars arriving and slowing to a stop, making the tail longer.

"Ah, damn, I told you! Maybe you can back up—!"

Kay grinned. "You know that button? The one I told you not to push?"

"Yeah?"

"You can push it now."

Jay glanced down at the covered button. He shook his head, thumbed the cover up. Said, "It ain't gonna do us no good to put on a siren or flash lights, they can't get out of the way! I rolled on patrol enough to know that."

"Just push the button, okay?"

"Fine." He mashed his thumb on the button, hard. "So this is how it ends. Cooked by an alien phaser beam in a crappy damned LTD sitting next to a redneck in a black suit." He shook his head. "My mother would be so proud."

The car . . . burbled.

The LTD rumbled, then thrummed as if some giant cat had waked up and started to purr.

"What the hell is that?"

"Might want to make sure your seat belt is snugged down tight there, sport."

Jay felt as much as saw the LTD begin to change. The sides kind of pushed out, the back end got longer, the smooth metal surfaces developed ridges. It took a second for Jay to take it in. Looked as if the car had sprouted muscles, steel lumps connected to each other by cablelike tendons, all of it sort of . . . pulsing and shining.

As if the LTD had suddenly morphed and turned into some kind of . . . metallic *animal*.

The hair on his neck rose. Goose bumps frosted him. This wasn't a stock Ford here.

At the moment, he didn't have time to marvel over it, because:

A panel truck loomed in front of them.

Kay was doing seventy, easy, and in another second, he was going to slam into that truck hard enough to turn it and them and maybe a couple more cars ahead into a big smoking *accordian*. Going to be one hellacious traffic jam *then*—

"Oh, *shiiit!*" Jay said. He stomped his foot onto an imaginary brake, trying to halt the car. "Stop! We're gonna die!"

Kay whipped the wheel toward the right and the LTD swerved.

Not going to do any good, there was no place to go, it was a goddamned *tunnel!* Jay could see it in his mind's eye: They'd hit, spin off that wall, and twist like a bullet until they came down on top of the line of traffic and crunched into a flaming LTD of death!

If they were *lucky*—!

There came from under the car a kind of sucking sound. Like nothing Jay had ever heard. He wanted to close his eyes so when the car plowed into the tunnel wall he wouldn't have to see himself go through the windshield, but he couldn't even blink, his eyes were wide, frozen open like carved from stone.

Going to *die* now—!

The car swerved up onto the wall.

On to the wall.

They were at a right angle to the road, *down* was directly to Jay's left and the LTD just kept moving along the wall like a fly—a real fast fly. The car angled up further, corkscrewed, until it was on the ceiling, *upside down!* and still going along at speed.

Oh, man. No way.

Kay said, "Mind if I smoke?"

Jay was drooping in the seat belt, blood rushing to his head. Riding upside down on the ceiling of the Midtown Tunnel and this crazed man next to him was talking about cigarettes. "What?!"

"Smoke. In the car."

"I don't care if you smoke!"

"No need to get your shorts in a wad, sport. It's just common courtesy to ask. These days, some people don't like it when you light up in the car."

Kay swerved to avoid something sticking out of the ceiling, some kind of electrical fixture. Lit a cigarette, cracked the window to let the smoke out. "Used to be you could toke just about anywhere. Back when I started, most everybody smoked. Now, you got to get a permit to go out into your own backyard, got to file an environmental impact statement to have one lousy cigarette. Not even talking about cigars or pipes, that's another whole ball of wax."

Jay stared at him. His head pounded. His eyes throbbed.

"Course, I should quit, I know it's bad for you." He took another drag, exhaled blue-gray smoke from his nostrils. "You know the old joke. 'Hell, quitting is easy—I've done it five or six times!' That's the problem, it never took. I'd lay off for a day, a week, even a month, then things would get bad on the job—some Retob Neutral would run off with a Retob Positive, some Gregnog would accidentally eat a Fligparg, and next thing you know, I'd be lighting up again."

Jay blinked. His head was really starting to hurt from being upside down. Yoga had never been his thing.

"Makes me wonder if I lack control sometimes. Not enough self-discipline."

They were coming up on the end of the tunnel. What would happen when they ran out of ceiling?

Dismemberment. Disfigurement. Death . . .

"Kay," Jay began.

"Yeah?"

"Kay—!"

The LTD flew from the tunnel, twisted until it was flying above the traffic, then came down in an empty lane. It hit the ground no harder than coming off a speed bump.

Kay rolled the window down, snapped the cigarette out through the open window with his thumb and forefinger. It left an orange streak. "I really do have to quit," he said.

The toll booths loomed. There was only one of them open and it looked like it was nine lanes in the wrong direction.

The LTD shot across the lanes at what Jay figured was no more than three or four times the speed limit. Okay, maybe five times.

Kay flipped a token out through the still-open window. Jay saw the token fall into the basket as the LTD smashed through the gate.

Kay smiled at Jay's reaction. "Timing, it's all in the timing. Well, okay, a little wrist action, but mostly, you let the speed of the vehicle do the work, you know?"

"You're crazy. You are crazy. Crazy."

"Probably so. Listen, I'm gonna have to step on it," Kay said. "Hang on."

"*Step* on it? What are you talking about, step on it? We got to be doing a hundred now!"

Kay grinned wider. "One-thirty," Kay said. "But hell, son, I only got my foot halfway to the floor. This baby'll do two and a half if I fill it with superpremium. Maybe two-seventy if the wind is behind it. I hardly ever get to open her up, and time is of the essence, remember?"

"Oh, shit!"

"You remember this next time you disrespect a man's car, hey?"

Jay nodded dumbly. He would. He surely would. If he lived long enough to remember anything.

Outside, things were a blur. The LTD, now more steel tiger than car, ran at a speed a high-category hurricane would envy.

"Boy, we having fun now, ain't we?" Kay said.

Jay struggled to find his cool. It must be back there in

187

the tunnel somewhere, probably gonna take a while to catch up, but he tried. "Oh, yeah. Fun. You think I can drive next time? You poke along like an old woman."

Kay smiled. "You doing all right, Jay. For a new guy."

When she was a little girl, Laurel had owned a Barbie doll. And a Ken and a Malibu beach house and probably several hundred dollars' worth of other Barbie stuff she'd begged her parents to buy her.

Her year-older jerk of a brother, William Daniel, called "BD" by his retarded twerp friends, had been into sci fi. One day while she was playing in the tree house with her friend Elizabeth, BD had gone into her room and kidnapped Barbie and Ken. By the time Laurel found out, BD had already gone out into the summer sunshine and subjected Barbie to the "alien death ray"—a big magnifying glass. He'd singed her beautiful blond hair off, melted big holes in her, then he had sliced her in half. It must have taken a long time, even as big as the magnifying glass was.

Barbie was a smoldering, stinking ruin when

20

BD decided the alien invaders had dealt with her enough and started on Ken.

When she found him with Barbie, Laurel was so enraged that she wanted nothing more than to kill her brother. The only weapon at hand was the garden hose. She picked it up and swung the end of it like a stick, clonked BD on the top of the head with the hose's metal nozzle, and split his scalp open enough to require twelve stitches.

It was the day after the Fourth of July and the emergency room had been full of waiting patients with hands blasted by firecrackers and burned by sparklers, plus a busful of people from a church picnic where the potato salad had gone bad. People were puking everywhere, kids were yelling, and her brother was making as much noise as anybody.

Her parents had not been pleased.

That was the day Laurel decided to become a doctor. Not to help her idiot brother, but to fix Barbie.

Unfortunately, Barbie was dead and beyond the skills of even the best doll doctor to repair. Ken was in better shape, but with melted black holes where he'd had eyes. She gave him some sunglasses and a white cane, got a new Barbie—which BD had to pay for out of his allowance—but things were never quite the same. She had on that day, and in the weirdest way, learned about death. Barbie had been real to her, and she had died, and the new Barbie was not the same person.

Now, as Laurel stood next to a creature from another planet, she felt the cold and stinking breath of death again, and in a way unlike her job, where she dealt with death every day.

This was personal. This *thing* had said it was going to eat her. How it was going to get off Earth, she couldn't begin to say. Why it wanted to come to the World's Fair site didn't make any sense, either, but here they were.

She was not ready to end up an alien's entree. She had to do something, but damned if she could figure out what.

Edgar stood at the base of the Permarian ship tower, the female next to him. He supposed that putting the ships right out in public on display was actually a fairly clever way to hide them—from terrans, at least. Anybody who had ever been off this one-rocket world would recognize them immediately, Permarian design being considered a classic in some circles. Especially the '55 model. But, of course, these lowlife meat sacks wouldn't know a classic if, well—if you put one up on a post for the entire world to see. And not just one, but *two* of them.

Amazing.

The female said, "Listen, you don't want to eat me. I wouldn't taste very good. Besides, I'm a very important person on my world. Kind of like a . . . queen. Even a goddess. There are those who worship the ground I walk upon. I'm not telling you this to be bragging, you understand, just to warn you. Eating me might start a war. Almost surely would."

"Good," Edgar said. "War means food and wealth for my family. All seventy-eight million of them. That's a lot of mouths to feed, Your Highness."

"Seventy-eight million? My, you must take a lot of vitamins. And I'm sure you're a wonderful father," she said. "Maybe we can negotiate something? A food drop? A low-interest loan?"

"Up," he said. "Climb."

"Why?"

"Because I will kill you if you do not."

"Okay, since you put it that way."

The female preceded him up the tower.

As she climbed, she talked. "No offense, but you know you're beginning to rot around the edges?"

They ascended the tower. Edgar said, "The disguise has served its purpose."

"Disguise?"

"You don't think I ordinarily look like this? It is beyond me how you can stand yourselves. Internal skeleton, meat on the outside? If you had any idea how hideous you really were, you'd all kill yourselves."

"You get used to it," the female said. "Oh, have you seen this?"

Edgar paused and looked up. He was beneath the female. She lifted one of her legs, drew it back toward her . . .

Then kicked him square in the face.

The force was insignificant, but the surprise did cause him to lose his concentration momentarily. He had to make sure his grip did not slip and as he did so, the female took advantage of this to fling herself from the tower.

He lunged, grabbed at her as she fell past, but missed.

Well, rabnaz dung!

The expected fall and subsequence bursting open of the fleshy creature when she splattered against the ground did not occur, however. Instead, she fell into the branches of one of those tall woody plants. A number of the tree's branches cracked or broke under her weight, but there was sufficient foliage to slow her descent so that part of the way down, she was able to grab a large limb and stop completely. Still shy of the ground by several times her own height. She pulled herself up onto the limb and perched upon it. Looked at Edgar. Smiled.

Well. They were born of the trees, weren't they? It wasn't so amazing they could still play around in them, was it?

Edgar considered going back down the tower to fetch the female. It *was* a long flight to the nearest civilized outpost. On the other feeler, he wasn't particularly hungry and could no doubt make it another few weeks or months without feeding. Probably the Permarian food processor could make sugar if he programmed it right. And if he got a bad case of the munchies, well, there was always the disguise, wasn't there? True, it was pretty ripe, but it would do in a pinch. And he needed to get off this planet quickly. Another "meteor" would doubtless be coming soon, and he did not wish to be here when it arrived.

He sighed. All right. So, let the human go. It was no chitin off his knees. He had a family to get back to, no time to dally here any longer.

He scurried up the tower, moving much faster now that the human wasn't blocking his path.

Laurel could not believe she'd done something so stupid. Just jumped off a tower like that. Yeah, she'd seen the tree, and yeah, it was her plan—such that it was—to let the tree break her fall, but, boy, that was iffy. She could have easily wound up on a table waiting for her replacement to slice her open and see what was what, and wouldn't that have been embarrassing?

Still—it had worked, hadn't it? She was alive, the alien monster didn't show any signs of coming back to get her. And better to break her neck falling, where she at least had a chance, than to get *eaten* by a space creature. Among all the ways to die, that one had never even made the list. Who would have considered such a thing?

She had to wonder. What did monstro there think it was going to *do* in that display? Was there, like, a mother ship going to beam him up from there? Surely it—he, whatever—didn't think that model saucer was *real*?

Then again, who cared what it thought? She was alive, albeit up a tree, and the bug-eyed monster was going in another direction. Things could be a lot worse.

Now, she needed to gather herself together and climb down from here and get the hell away. Now.

Kay slid the now-reverted LTD to a skidding stop in the empty parking lot outside the World's Fair site. Kay jumped out, ran to the trunk. Jay was right behind him.

It was a pretty big damned trunk. You could get in and lie down, Jay thought, wasn't for all the crap Kay had in the thing.

Kay grabbed a long black box, unsnapped a row of latches, flipped the lid open—

Man, look at that. Had to be the most wicked-looking gun he'd ever seen. Had three barrels, over, under, and under, an easy three feet long, with a pump-action reloader and a storage magazine looked like it would hold a dozen extra rounds of ammo. And the ammo, it looked like shotgun shells made out of stainless steel, big, nasty rounds glistening in the LTD's trunk light.

Jay wondered what happened when you pulled the trigger and let one of those shells loose. Nothing good for whatever was on the receiving end, he was pretty sure.

Kay started feeding rounds into the magazine.

"You know how to use that?"

Kay jacked a shell from the magazine into the chamber, *chunk-chunk!* Said, "No idea. I'll just have to wing it. Take that Pulsar Rifle."

Jay picked up an only-slightly-less-evil-looking longarm from the trunk. "This?"

"Yes."

For a second, Jay felt better. Gun like this ought to knock a tank over. Then again, the Noisy Cricket had surprised the hell out of him, too—

"Close the trunk. The clock is running here."

Jay slammed the trunk closed. Looked up and saw the saucer towers. Heard something weird. A humming, going up in pitch.

"What's that?"

"Crap," Kay said. "Look."

One of the saucers started to spin, like a gyroscope balanced on a pencil. Lights gleamed from some kind of array around the outside.

"Oh, man! We're too late!"

"Come on!"

They ran.

Edgar waved his hands over the ship's controls, was pleased to see that nearly all systems were active. Lights sparkled over the board. A recorded announcement, in Permarian, played:

"Passengers are advised to please extinguish all smoking materials and engage their stasis couch controls for takeoff."

This was followed by Permarian music, an awful cacophony that would gag a spugor. Hurriedly Edgar shut off the sound. Later he would see if there were any passable tunes in the storage system, something more suited to a decent species. He did not hold out a lot of hope for that, since it was well known that Permarian musical tastes were generally putrid, and that their own music was the worst from any known species. Well. Save perhaps for some of the newer terran so-called music he had heard while searching for

21

the galaxy. Rock and roll? Reggae? Rap? Stomach churning, all of it . . .

Enough. He would have plenty of time to fiddle with entertainment systems once he was off-planet. He was practically home free, best not to linger now. In a few minutes, this world was going to be a bad memory, cut into smoking trash by yet another exchange in the Arquillian-Baltian Conflict. Time he got home, the war should be in full swing again, and everybody in the family would feed well. Other families would benefit, too, not that anybody from them would give him the least bit of credit, oh, no. Well, that was the way of it. Trickle-down economics. He didn't care if they ate, long as his own family was fed.

Edgar engaged the saucer's lift. There came a powerful hum as the integrated engines rumbled and came on-line. Ninety-eight percent power available. How long had the ship been perched here? Ah, those Permarians, you had to give it to them, they knew how to build a decent ride!

One of the disguise's fingers fell off. Oh, well. He could hardly wait to get out of the damned costume. Soon as he cleared the gravity well, he was going to shuck Edgar and get back to his beautiful self. One could stand only so much ugliness.

Ah, the things one did for one's family.

In that, the human female had been right. The responsibilities of being a father demanded much and he *was* a good father, if he did say so himself. Better than most. He'd like to see Merg or Barl or even Revo stuffed into one of these human suits for ten heartbeats. They'd go mad and start trashing everything they could lay a pincher on, he was sure of it, and Demons take their families. Not him. He knew where his duties lay. He did what was necessary, loathsome as it was at times. He might have had to do worse in the past than this, but offpincher, he couldn't remember so doing.

Never mind. It was almost over.

The shipcraft rose from the platform, tore loose with a satisfying *crunch* from the molding that held the ship in place.

So long, fleshboys.

Kay skidded to a stop, cursing with a fluency that a carrier full of sailors would no doubt envy. "He's lifted!"

"What do we do?"

Kay raised his triple-barreled shotgun. Looked at Jay. "It's a long shot but we got nothing to lose. Set your rifle to pulsar level five, subsonic implosion factor four—"

"Say what?"

"The green button. Press the little green button. Line up on the saucer, then on three, we pull the triggers, okay?"

Jay nodded. He could handle that. He aimed the rifle at the saucer. There was a ghost ring sight on the end of the barrel and he centered it on the rising craft. He pressed the arming button. "I'm ready."

"All right. One . . . two . . . *three!*"

Jay pulled the trigger on his weapon.

For a second, it seemed the guns must have misfired. Nothing happened. Then there was a *thump!* kind of like thunder, as if a lot of air rushed in to fill a big vacuum in a big hurry. Jay felt, then saw a tremendous shock wave roll out from their vicinity, a kind of distortion in the air, as it raced wavelike toward the saucer. The recoil of the wave slapped the two of them down, hard. They hit the

ground on their bellies. Jay tried to lift himself, couldn't.
Managed to get his face raised a little, enough to see the
shock wave reach the saucer and . . .

. . . *suck it down.*

Heading right toward them—

"Dammit—!"

Jay tried to close his eyes, but they didn't want to
work that way. Gonna crush them like bugs—

Edgar felt the pulse hit the ship, felt the lift go, knew
almost instantly what had happened.

He cursed loudly and repeatedly. The tragvilian
wuper scum had contraband weapons! What kind of
ruynanese qirt-kissing binju-licking doop would give terrans that kind of gear? There were laws! Didn't anybody
have any morality these days?

The ship fell.

Was nothing sacred?

Apparently not—

Laurel would have yelled at the two men but some invis-
ible force shook the tree as they fired those strange
weapons at the departing saucer.

How could a damned display do that? Fly?

Never mind that—some slopover of whatever it was
they shot blew through the branches and the tree moved
as if a giant had grabbed it and was trying to shake her
out of it. She clutched the trunk with both arms,
wrapped her legs around it.

Even so, it was a near thing. Branches broke and fell,
leaves showered every which way, her teeth rattled and
clicked as she clung to the trunk.

When the storm eased, Laurel looked at the men. They were flat on the ground, but the cute, not-too-bright one was coming up and yelling. She couldn't make it out, but he was also pointing at the saucer, so she looked that way.

The saucer was flying, or maybe falling, right at her.

She would have screamed but her voice had somehow shorted out. She managed a squeak, that was all.

This was not right. Maybe it was all some kind of nightmare? Maybe she was home in bed, asleep, and none of this was happening?

Maybe. But she didn't believe that. The rough bark under her hands, the smells and sounds, they seemed too real to be a dream. That was only wishful thinking.

The saucer fell . . .

Kay watched as the saucer wobbled, fell. It looked like it was going to land right on top of them, but that was an illusion—if the kid had set his gun right.

He sure *hoped* the kid had set his gun right.

Apparently he had. The saucer dropped and crashed well short of them, into the Unisphere, that big old steel globe, splashing up metal, concrete foundation, dirt.

Maybe the stasis couch didn't work, that would save everybody the cost of a trial—

They should be so lucky. As he and the kid came up and ran that way, Kay watched the hatch slide back as the man who looked more and more like Frankenstein's monster every time they saw him appeared in the hatchway.

Kay lifted his weapon, aimed it.

"Stupid meat sacks! It doesn't matter! I've already won!"

He hopped out of the ship and started walking toward them.

Part of his face fell off. Just a little piece.

"Hold it right there, bug. You are under arrest for violating Section Two, Article four-dash-one-dash-fifty-three of the Tycho Accord. Please hand over any galaxy you might be carrying."

"Milk-sucking fleshboy! You don't matter. In a few minutes, you won't even *be* matter! You can't stop it! I know the warships are up there!"

"Fine. Just give me an excuse to cook you a little early, bug! Now, move away from the vehicle and put your hands on top of your head," Kay ordered. He waved the gun.

"Put my hands on top of my head?"

He grinned.

Kay tightened his grip on the gun. A grinning bug, that was a bad sign. He wanted to cook the bug, right now, but at this range, a blast might vaporize the target and somewhere, the bug had the galaxy. Probably wouldn't do their cause any good if he disintegrated the galaxy along with the bug. No, shooting him wouldn't be such a good idea.

Kay hoped the bug wouldn't realize that.

Finally, Edgar thought. Finally, at last, he was going to get to get rid of this ugly disguise!

He took a deep breath.

A real deep breath . . .

Jay didn't know if the green-button setting was the right one—he wasn't even the least bit interested in sucking the bug over here into his face given how he'd seen him move and all—but he didn't know which other control to use, so he just held the rifle pointed at Edgar like he knew what he was doing.

He didn't much like the way Edgar smiled at them. Bug ought not to be grinning in a situation like this, no sir.

The bug flexed his arms. The skin burst and he extended what looked like huge cockroach legs to the sides.

Damn, he had to have a twenty-foot reach!

The clothes, then the flesh on Edgar's legs ripped, revealed two more hideous-looking insect legs, doubled over a couple of times. The legs unfolded and the bug raised himself up to his full height. Which was very tall.

Jay had to crane his neck to see the thing's head—

Even as he was growing taller, his torso split, his head exploded, and in the space of two heartbeats, Edgar was . . . gone.

Little scraps of him lay here and there like a popped balloon, but nothing recognizable as human.

What stood in Edgar's place was a giant, hairy bug with a long, scaly tail tipped by a wicked, needle-pointed stinger. His head looked kind of like a cobra's, with elliptical eyes and a tiny nose, and his feet were three-toed and kind of like a camel's.

Ugly? He was uglier than an NBA pro basketball player in a tight pink dress.

Jay could smell the poison dripping from the creature's stinger. Smelled like crushed ants. Several hundred thousand crushed ants, maybe.

"Oh, *shit*," Jay said.

The bug put its roach arms on top of its head. "Hands on my head? Like this?"

Jay looked at Kay.

"Now what?" Jay said.

"He moves, blast him."

"Really?" the bug said. "Blast me? I think not."

"You think wrong, bug," Kay said. "Twitch and you get turned into superheated steam! Won't be enough of you left to fill up a teacup!"

"You bluff, terran. If it was just me standing here, I bet you'd do it in a Cemonian second, but I know you won't. You know how I know? Because there are un-counted billions at risk, aren't there, monkey man? You understand what I'm talking about, don't you?"

Jay glanced at Kay. "He's talking about the galaxy," Jay said.

"I *know* what he's talking about," Kay responded.

To the bug, Kay said, "Listen up, roach breath, I might not be able to blow you away but I sure as hell can take you off at the knees. Might be painful."

The bug laughed. Said, "Pain? What kind of threat is that? If you can't kill me, who cares? I can grow new legs. Besides, how do you know I don't have the galaxy in a knee pocket? It could be anywhere on me, couldn't it? You can't take the risk, can you?"

Kay didn't respond.

"Got ourselves a Rexigan standoff, don't we, meat sack?"

This sucker was *huge!* Jay felt like a guppy facing off against a Great White shark. Jay wasn't sure what this gun would do if he shot it, but if bug-boy over there twitched a feeler, they were both sure gonna find out, galaxy or no galaxy.

The bug *spat* on them.

It happened so fast Jay couldn't believe it. All of a sudden a gob of sticky goo the size of a couple of basketballs just . . . shot out and landed on Jay's hands and arms and weapon. The goo was connected to the bug by a long, drooping, ropy tentacle of the stuff. Jay tried to pull the trigger but before he could, the bug . . . inhaled and sucked the goo back into its mouth.

Taking with it Jay and Kay's weapons, along with some skin off their hands. And Jay's fake Rolex.

"Uh-oh," Kay said.

22

Jay realized that it would be better to be someplace else and he started to move, but the bug—he was fast for a big alien—whipped one of its roach arms out and swept both men off their feet and a good fifteen feet through the air, to land sprawling.

"I got your 'Hands on your head' right here, meat sacks!" the bug said.

It clacked those big clawlike pinchers and it sounded like a giant snapping a telephone pole in half.

"Now what?" Jay said, as he scrambled to his feet. "This ain't goin' exactly like we planned."

"This guy is really starting to piss me off," Kay said. He brushed dirt off his suit.

"Can you use the neuralyzer? Make him forget who he is?"

"Doesn't work on bugs."

"Any other tricks in your bag?"

"I don't suppose you've still got the Noisy Cricket?"

Jay said, "Son-of-a-bitch, yeah!" He slapped at his coat pocket.

Empty.

"Damn," Jay said. "Must have fallen out somewhere."

"We don't have time to look for it right now." Kay stared at the bug, which just stood there watching them. Jay couldn't be sure but he thought the bug was grinning. Probably enjoying the hell out of itself. Abruptly, the bug turned around and started toward the ship. Kay started after it.

"Where are you going?"

"Got to get my gun back."

"How? You gonna stick your finger down its throat and make it puke? It *ate* the goddamned guns, Kay!"

"Whatever happens, don't let it get on that ship."

Jay stared at him. "How am I supposed to do that? Try to reason with it?"

"Why not? It could die laughing."

Kay went after the bug. Jay glanced around, looking for his gun, for a rock, a stick, anything he could use.

Kay yelled. "Hey, bug! Where are you going?"

The bug didn't pause.

"Hey, I'm talking to you! You know how many of your kind I've swatted with a rolled-up newspaper?"

The bug stopped. Turned. Loomed over Kay like an insect version of a Tyrannosaurus rex.

Kay said, "You're nothing more than a greasy smear on the sports page, pal! A slimy, dung-eating, intestinal parasite!" Kay grabbed his crotch like a ballplayer adjusting his jewels. "Eat me!"

The bug hissed. Sounded to Jay like a yard full of steam locomotives. Cranked its mouth open—Geez-us, it was like a snake, it could unhinge its jaws!—leaned down and did just that.

It ate Kay.

Sucked him into its maw, leaned its head back, and swallowed him whole.

Jay saw Kay's whole body slide down the creature's gullet, saw the thing's throat distend like a snake ingesting a rat as Kay's elbows and knees worked, pushing against the inside. Heard Kay's muffled scream as he disappeared.

Oh, *man!*

The bug reared to its full height—it really was a monster—and roared. Sounded like a tornado ripping up a trailer park.

Game over, Jay thought. Time to boogie. No way was he going to be dessert.

But the bug's stomach wasn't covered with an exoskeleton, it was more like stiff leather. And inside the thing, Jay saw the outline of one of the guns it had sucked down. And—

—what looked like a hand groping toward the weapon.

Damn!

The bug turned back toward the ship.

Jay knew he had to act fast. He ran, angled past the bug, toward the rubble created by the crashed ship. Found a chunk of concrete half the size of a bowling ball, hefted it. He took a short run to get up some momentum, then flung the missile.

It hit the bug on the shell part of one hip and bounced off.

Damn.

Jay looked around. Spotted a twisted section of metal, a pole about his own height and as thick as his wrist. He picked it up, circled around behind the bug as it neared the saucer.

"Stop right there, bug, or I'm gonna whale on your waxy ass!"

The bug ignored him. Paused to let out a terrific belch, then began working on the saucer, clearing crap away from the base.

Jay whacked the bug with the metal pole. Hit it again and again. Sounded like a man banging on the side of a fifty-five-gallon oil drum full of liquid.

Laurel couldn't believe what she was seeing. It just kept getting weirder and weirder. She was gonna to need a new word. The alien popped his human disguise and expanded into a giant roach, grew by a factor of five, maybe more, poof! just like that. Then it spat some kind of snot at the two men, caught their weapons, sucked them down its maw.

Then it ate one of the guys.

She had to get down out of this tree. She had to do it now and get as far away from here as she could as fast as she could. Even Queens after dark wasn't this scary. The local thugs might do awful things to you, even kill you, but they probably wouldn't eat you afterward.

Climb, girl, climb!

She started down the tree, scraping her hands and legs and face, but that didn't matter. The scratches would heal, assuming you weren't being digested in the belly of a bug bigger than an elephant.

Go, go!

Kerb—he no longer had to think of himself as the Edgar now, thank any and all the gods—paused in his excavation of the saucer. Perhaps he should just climb the other tower and take the second ship?

No, better to use this one. It was closer, he was in a hurry, and that little fall shouldn't have damaged it.

He became aware of a rhythmic gonging sound. He turned.

There, far below, the dark human stood, pounding on his carapace with a metal implement. Kerb felt a pang of amusement. Had to give them credit for bravery, if not for brains. He reached down, grabbed the metal pole, and pulled.

The human let go. Good idea, otherwise he would have been flung as far as Kerb could fling such a being, a not inconsiderable distance in his present form.

Kerb swung the metal stick at the human. Missed as it dropped to the ground. He tossed the stick away, drove a pincher at the human. It rolled to the side and all he got was a claw full of concrete. Bah!

Jay rolled under the bug. If it sat, he was going to be road kill. He saw a twisted strip of steel, a piece of rebar shorn off into a short, sharp spike. He grabbed it. The underbelly was soft. A good jab and maybe he could let some of the air out of this sucker's tires!

The bug pivoted on those huge legs, bent forward like one of those little toys that bobs and drinks water out of a cup, and all of a sudden, Jay found himself staring into the bug's upside-down face.

"What are you doing down there, fleshboy?"

Jay backed up in a hurry as the bug snapped at him with those incredible jaws. He rolled out from beneath the tail and came up, sprinted for all he was worth.

Finally, Kerb thought, the little pest has come to its senses.

He went back to his work on the ship. Cleared away a large chunk of building material.

Uh-oh. A rent in the hull! Blast! This wasn't supposed to happen to a Permarian ship! Shoddy workmanship abounded!

Oh, well. There was another ship. Best he get to it quickly.

He started away from the wreckage.

Jay was running out of options. Kay was still alive inside the bug and if he could get his hands on the gun before the thing's stomach bile cooked him, they had a chance.

He had to slow it down, somehow.

Jay ran, gathered himself, and tackled the bug.

Well, he launched himself onto one of the legs and grabbed it, but for all the effect it had, he might as well have been a flea on a big dog.

"You might be a bad ass back in your local hive, sucker, but this is New York City! You're just another tourist here! Stop!"

Jay lost his grip as the bug sped up. Managed to grab the tail, fortunately well above the stinger.

"I said, 'Stop!' You gonna be sorry if you don't!"

Laurel was almost close enough to the ground to jump, just a few more feet. She wasn't in that much of a hurry. It would not do to sprain an ankle and not be able to run real fast, no, unh-unh.

As she got lower into the thicker branches, she'd lost sight of the fight—if you could call it that—between the young guy and the bug. She could only catch a glimpse through the foliage now and then. The guy was yelling at the bug and banging on it with something and for his trouble, getting his butt thrown around pretty good.

He was either the bravest man she'd ever seen or a lot stupider than she had thought, which was hard to believe.

She wouldn't have gone up against that thing when it looked human. No way would she be chasing it now.

Kerb looked back. There it was again, the little meat sack, holding on to his tail. Had they not the intelligence of a stone, these humans?

Apparently not.

He flicked his tail, hard. Sent the little human flying through the air and turned away before the thing even landed. *No time to play any more, terry. I have places to go.*

Jay came down in the middle of a dumpster and fortunately, the rotting garbage was soft enough to break his fall without killing him. He got to his feet as well as he could, shook banana peels out of his hair, wiped something that smelled like week-old puke off his face.

He was out of options here.

He looked down as a roach scuttled down his arm. Shit! He flicked the roach off. Looked down, and saw dozen more of the cockroaches, some as long as his thumb, disturbed by his sudden arrival. Bugs. Everywhere, bugs!

This is not your biggest concern here now, is it, Jay? A few ordinary bugs ain't nothing when you got an infestation like Edgar! Or what had been Edgar.

Suddenly an idea came to him.

He looked down, kicked at the side of the rusted dumpster. The metal was thin and it gave. Garbage spilled out, and a horde of roaches went with it, flowing like a dark brown stream. Jay heaved himself over the edge of the dumpster, came down in the middle of the roiling roaches.

Yeeww!

There's nothing that sounds quite like stepping on a roach. It's a kind of brittle crunch that, once you've heard it, you never forget it. Jay had grown up hearing it. No matter how much his parents sprayed their place with bug poison, there were always a few resistant cucarachas who survived to get stepped on. It embarrassed

211

his mother to no end that she had such creatures. His father said they must have come up from Mississippi in her grandmother's old cedar chest and he couldn't understand how they thrived in Pennsylvania, but whatever their source, they were there to stay. Some months Jay's mother only caught a few in the traps or saw a couple that crawled out of the walls to die, but they never went away altogether.

In his former apartment, the roaches would break down the roach traps and haul them away, eat the poison dust and lick the plate. No, the only way to be sure the suckers were dead was to step on them and listen for the crunch.

The departing alien, already starting to climb the tower, stopped. Nothing wrong with its ears, apparently.

"Hey, check it out, bug! Wasn't that your *cousin* I just crushed?"

The bug turned around. It did not look happy. "What did you say?"

Well, Jay. You got its full attention. Now what?

The thing to do, Jay realized, was to keep the bug's attention.
And apparently he did not like the idea of Jay
squashing his distant kin.

Jay moved over a hair, raised his foot, brought
it down on a big roach.

Maybe the sound was kind of like stepping on
a fresh potato chip? No, it was louder than that.
Stomping on a Frito? Closer. Not exactly, but
not too far off. Distinctive, for sure.

Jay said, "Oops. You believe in reincarnation?
Why, that little devil might come back as your
new nephew. Then again, maybe he already *was*
your nephew."

The alien glowered at him. "Do not do that,"
he said. But he didn't move from his position on
the tower.

Jay danced to his left. Did a little heel and toe

23

and came down, caught two of the roaches together. *Crunch! Crunch!*

Jay said, "And there goes Uncle John and Aunt Sally! What? What's that? Hey, ugly, can't you hear your little kinfolk over here? They're yelling, 'Help me! Help me!' "

"Cease," the bug said.

Jay grinned. Moved over a hair. Looked down at the roaches. "Sorry, Sundance, Butch can't help you. Your number is up. Oh, my, check out *this* one. She's a beauty. Why, I do believe she looks familiar. Don't you think so? Hey, hey, I know who she is!"

The bug climbed down from the tower and marched toward Jay. Well, as much as a giant alien can march.

"Yep, yep, I recognize her, all right. Family resemblance is downright amazing!"

"If you have gods, best you pray to them, fleshboy. Your moment has come."

Jay brought his foot down, hard. *Crunch!*

"Say adios! It's your *mama*, bug!"

"Speak not of my mother, skort-face!"

The bug moved, mouth open to inhale Jay as it had Kay. But this time, it was showing a lot of teeth. Maybe it intended to chew on him before it gulped him down. That would be bad. Even going down in a lump like Kay would be bad.

Bad all around here.

Jay held his position. Not that he had anywhere to go, anyhow.

"So long, human scum!"

Jay drew his fist back. Might as well go down swinging—

The bug exploded.

Well, not all of him. Just his midsection. But it was

enough so he blew into two large pieces, a top and bottom, and the spray of bug guts, leather belly, and whatever else hit Jay like a warm and putrid shower. The top half of the bug flew a few feet and hit the ground; the bottom half did a couple of rolls and stopped under a nearby tree.

"Eeww!" Jay yelled. He wiped his eyes. Felt as if he'd been hit in the face with a bug cream pie.

Kay climbed out of the bottom section of blown-up bug after it jittered to a halt. He was likewise somewhat the worse for wear and considerably gooey. Looked like he'd been slimed. He dropped the three-barreled shotgun and staggered toward Jay, wiping green crap—probably *real* crap, come to think of it—from his face.

"You miss me?" Kay said.

"You get my rifle while you were in there?" Jay said.

"Up yours," Kay said.

"I can't believe you did that," Jay began. "That was your plan? Getting *eaten*?"

"Worked, didn't it?"

"You bastard—"

Kay held a finger up to his lips and shushed Jay. Pulled his cell phone from his inside pocket, shook a little goo off of it. In his other hand, he held a tiny bauble. He waved it at Jay, tapped a button on his phone.

"Zed? Kay. We got the bug *and* we got the galaxy. You might want to get on the horn to the A's and B's, tell them to hold off. Yeah, right. Uh-huh. Sure." He broke the connection.

"What'd he say?"

"Said he had the battle wagons on the line. They're willing to hold off long enough to send somebody to check this out." He held the galaxy up again. "Also said to pick him up one of those soft pretzels on the way in. He really likes those."

Jay sensed rather than saw what happened next. Felt a sense of sudden dread envelop him. Spun—

—saw the top half of the bug, levered up on its arms, mouth open, about to fall on them.

"Oh, *shit!*"

Kerb dragged his upper half toward the humans. It was going to strain his regeneration capabilities to their utmost to survive this one. Maybe he wouldn't make it. Truth was, he didn't know any of his species who'd lost their whole bottom half and come back, but he was tough. There was always a first time.

Whatever, he had to kill these damned humans. At the very least, if he was going to cross over the Bridge to the Other Side, he was not going without the company of those who'd sent him there.

He lifted himself, opened his mouth. Now—!

Jay screamed, something wordless, and prepared to die—

Boom! The bug's head shattered, blew apart. Bits of chitin and brain and circulating fluid splashed and pattered all over Jay and Kay, organic shrapnel.

"God*dammit!*" Jay yelled. "I'm getting *tired* of this! I'm *never* gonna get this crap off me!" He slung slime and goo from his hands.

Both men turned. Saw Laurel there, the other atomizer in her hands. As they watched, she dropped the weapon and wiped bug digestive juices off on her shirt.

"Where did you come from?" Jay said.

"Well, White Plains, originally," she said. She grinned. "But lately, I spent a little time up in that tree, watching you dance with Gruesome there. Interesting job you boys have. You going to tell me what this is all about?"

Jay and Kay looked at each other. "It's kind of a long story," Jay said.

"I have some time off coming," Laurel said. "Take as long as you want. I can't wait to hear this."

Laurel stood in front of the two men, still amazed at all she had seen. It had been her intent to hit the ground running, but when the cut-in-half creature rolled over and disgorged that weapon, it had been almost right under the tree.

Before she could drop, the thing moved, not dead in the least, and started for the two men. The gun was right there as she came down and she couldn't just take off and leave them to get chomped on, could she?

She hadn't fired a gun since an ex-boyfriend had taught her how to shoot apartment mice in his Village loft with an air rifle and this wasn't exactly a BB gun, but the worst she could do was miss and they wouldn't be any deader if she did.

It was a lucky shot, but they didn't have to know that.

The young one grinned at her. "Hi," he said. "My name is Jay."

The drive back into Manhattan was uneventful. More or less.
Some fool tried to pass Kay on a curve and Kay
ran him into a ditch. He was in no mood, he
said.

They told Laurel they would fill her in, but
they had to get clearance from their boss, first.
She seemed content to wait that long.

Once they got back to HQ, Jay started feeling
a little squirmy. He knew what Kay had in mind
and he didn't like it.

"Wait here a second, would you?" Jay told
Laurel. "My partner and I need to have a quick
conference."

She nodded. "I wouldn't leave for the
world."

So it was that Jay and Kay stood on the sidewalk about fifty feet away from where the LTD
was parked in front of HQ as Laurel leaned

against the side of the car, arms crossed, watching them.

Jay said, "Look, I know we have rules and all and I appreciate the situation, but she did save our bacon back there with the bug. Besides, I don't trust that neuralyzer. How many times can you zap somebody before they can't remember their own zip code?"

"Do you know what *your* zip code is?"

"No, but that's not the point."

Kay sighed. "It is a problem, ain't it?" He pulled the neuralyzer from his pocket, examined it. "I don't think the bug's digestive juices bothered it. Supposed to be shockproof and waterproof and like that. Comes with a thousand-year money-back guarantee."

"Come on, Kay. She only hangs out with dead people anyhow. Who's she gonna tell? We could wave national security at her or something. Look, I really like her."

Kay looked up.

"What?"

"The stars. Hard to see here, all the city glow."

"Excuse me?"

"It was pointed out to me not too long ago that we hardly ever look at the stars. I believe the man who told me that was right. Once you get into this biz, the stars don't have the same meaning they did before you know about aliens and battleships and stuff like that."

Jay saw Laurel push away from the LTD and start toward them. "Hey, guys? What's up?"

Kay tapped the neuralyzer against his palm.

"No way we can cut her some slack? You got to use that thing on her?"

Kay pulled his gaze away from the sky, looked at Jay. "I'm not going to use it on her. You're going to use it— on me."

"I beg your pardon?"

"You were right when you called Zed and me 'old guys.' I've been on the job long enough. I'm about to retire."

"Come on, man, I didn't really mean that."

"You're a good kid, Jay. Zed will hang on long enough to make sure you get trained right. And he'll do right by me. It's time to leave this party."

Laurel arrived. "Guys? Something going on here I should know?"

Kay pulled his sunglasses from his pocket, handed them to Laurel. "Here, put these on."

"Why?"

"Trust me." He held the neuralyzer up and pointed out the controls to Jay. "These are seconds, minutes, hours, days, weeks, months, years, all coded with the first two letters so you don't get confused, see?"

"Yeah."

"Always point this end at the subject."

"Guys?" Laurel said.

"Nice working with you, Jay. I think you're gonna do all right."

"What about—what about Laurel?"

"Gonna be up to you, sport. But consider this." Kay reached over, put his hand over Laurel's name tag so that all of it was covered but the first letter of her name.

Jay looked. Understood. "You think?"

"She's got what it takes. Got to be more interesting than stiffs."

Jay nodded. "Yeah, yeah."

"Okay. Let's get on with it."

"Kay . . ."

"I spent part of the evening down the gullet of an

interstellar cockroach. You think I *want* to remember that? Do it. It's already set for thirty years."

He handed Jay the neuralyzer. Smiled.

Laurel said, "Is somebody going to tell me what is going on?"

"Just a second," Jay said. He put his sunglasses on.

Pointed the device at Kay.

Pressed the button.

Jay stood at the newsstand, looking at the tabloid headlines. The summer was winding down, he'd learned a whole bunch of stuff from Zed in a real short time, and things were looking better. No more bugs, at least, the A's and B's had taken their galaxy and gone home. At least the world didn't depend on his next move. Not today, anyhow.

Now, he was doing a little research:

Met's Centerfielder says:
UFO MADE ME MISS HOME RUN BALL!

Another one said:

DETROIT HAS CAR THAT DEFIES GRAVITY!!

Secret Tests in New York Tunnel Revealed!

And a third one:

MAN AWAKENS FROM
THIRTY YEAR COMA!!
Returns to Girl He Left Behind

Jay picked up the third tabloid. The jump for the headline showed a picture of Kay, smiling at the woman Jay knew was Elizabeth Reston. He was holding out a bouquet of flowers, just like the ones he'd failed to deliver thirty years ago.

Jay grinned. He loved a happy ending.

He collected the other papers, paid the man, headed back toward the LTD.

Inside, Elle—formerly Laurel—sat in the passenger seat, sharp in her tailored black suit, short hair, patent leather shoes. She made the clothes look even better than he did, and, well, that was saying something.

Jay got in, passed the papers to her.

"We stopped here for *these*? C'mon."

"Best investigative reporters on the planet," Jay said.

"Uh-huh. Just like this car is a classic, right?"

"Don't be dissin' my car, it's got hidden talents. See that button there?"

"Yeah?"

"You don't want to push that unless I tell you."

He started the engine. Grinned at her.

Elle said, "Zed called. The high consulate of Regent-Nine is bugging him. He wants floor seats to the Knicks-Bulls game."

"Him and everybody else," Jay said. "Well, let's go talk to Dennis Rodman, it's his damn planet."

Jay put it in gear and pulled away from the curb.

Elle said, "So I have a philosophical question."

"Shoot."

"How long do we keep doing this? I mean, without letting the secret out?"

"Long as the neuralyzers work, I guess."

"Come on, Jay. You know what I mean."

He nodded. Yeah, he knew. He shook his head. "I don't know. Kay and I weren't together too long and not really much into policy, being kinda busy and all. We're just the street cops. I guess we just keep plugging the holes in the dike until somebody upstairs decides the world is ready to know there really are aliens among us."

She nodded.

"Hey, it's better than cutting up dead people, right?"

"So far."

They grinned at each other.

EPILOGUE

From a few hundred feet up, the LTD was just another car in a long line of cars and trucks on the jammed Manhattan street. . . .

From thousands of feet up in the thin clouds, Manhattan was but a part of a much larger urban and suburban sprawl. . . .

From miles up in the stratosphere, the East Coast of the United States was but part of a much larger landmass. . . .

From the hundreds of miles into the eosphere, North America was but a portion of the planet Earth. . . .

From thousands of miles beyond the moon, Earth was but a tiny blue and white ball hung in among the stars. . . .

From a few light-months, the solar system was but blips of light. . . .

From light-years, the Milky Way was but one of millions of such creamy galactic spirals, globes, and clusters. . . .

From the edge of the universe, the curve of a deep blue globe could be seen. . . .

And from a place beyond time and space, a distance too vast to measure, the universe was but a deep blue marble, resting on a patch of red dirt as the hand of a giant beyond size reached down, picked up the marble, and flicked it across the dirt, where it rolled, then slowed, slowed . . . and came a stop . . .

. . . among a collection of other colored marbles . . .

About the Author

Steve Perry is the author of dozens of science fiction and fantasy novels, including the *New York Times* bestselling novel *Shadows of the Empire*. He has also completed numerous teleplays for series and developed screenplays for feature films. Steve lives in Oregon with his wife, who publishes a small monthly newspaper.